MW00647538

STAR-CROSSED WITCH

MISS MATCHED MIDLIFE DATING AGENCY
BOOK ONE

DEANNA CHASE

Copyright © 2022 by Deanna Chase

Editing: Angie Ramey

Cover image: © Ravven

ISBN 978-1-953422-52-1

All rights reserved. No part of this publication may be reproduced, stored in, or introduced into a retrieval system, or transmitted in any form, or by any means (electronic, mechanical, photocopying, recording, or otherwise) without the prior written permission of both the copyright owner and the publisher of this book.

This book is a work of fiction. Names, characters, places, and incidents are products of the author's imagination or are used fictitiously. Any resemblance to actual events, locals, business establishments, or persons, living or dead, are entirely coincidental.

Bayou Moon Press, LLC

www.deannachase.com

Printed in the United States of America

ABOUT THIS BOOK

A Paranormal Women's Fiction Novel.

Welcome to Miss Matched Midlife Dating Agency, where Marion Matched is ready to help you find your soul mate.

When it comes to dating, Marion Matched has seen it all. She's the witch people call when they're fed up with unsolicited d*ck pics on their dating apps, being ghosted, or asked to do questionable things with their date's feet. She has the unique ability to just know when two people are perfect for each other. There's only ever been one person she hasn't been able to match—herself. And that's fine with her. She's never wanted to settle down anyway. Or at least that's what she tells herself when she runs into her recently divorced high school sweetheart in her new town of Premonition Pointe.

Marion doesn't have time to worry about her own dating life, anyway. She has a new business to set up, a reputation to prove, and an annoying ghost to shake. But when Marion hires a social media influencer to document her dating experiences with the agency, a vicious curse turns every date into a nightmare. Sabotaged and in danger of losing her new business, Marion will need the help of her newly acquired ghost, the Premonition Pointe coven, and the man who keeps asking her out to save her dating agency... and just maybe make a love connection she never thought she'd find.

CHAPTER 1

"*A* smidge to the left," I said, gazing at the Miss Matched Midlife Dating Agency sign Grace Valentine was holding in place above the front door of my new office.

"Perfect!" Iris, my business manager, exclaimed. She gave a firm nod and checked that task off her list. "Now we can go get lunch."

I chuckled. She'd been complaining she was starving for the last twenty minutes. "Sounds good. Just let me grab my laptop and phone so I can work on plumping up my database before the mixer next week."

"This space is so nice. It almost makes me wish I was single so you could set me up with my dream man," Grace said with a hand placed over her heart.

"That would've been too easy. Anyone with eyes can see in half a second that you and Owen are a perfect match," I said, winking at her.

Her lips curved into a small smile as her blue eyes sparkled.

1

"That's nice to hear, but I'm much more interested in what our auras say."

"Nope. No way. It's my firm policy to never comment on aura compatibility after a couple has already committed to each other. It's irrelevant since you've already chosen each other. Besides, your auras sort of merge after you've been together a while, so my radar isn't as useful." My special gift was reading auras and being able to match other people with their soul mates. The one time I told a friend that her aura wasn't compatible with her fiancé's, I not only lost that friend, but my thoughtless remark had been the catalyst for a lot of problems the couple eventually had to work out in therapy.

It wasn't for me to tell anyone who they shouldn't be with. The human heart had the ability to love whomever it wanted. My job was to help make the love match easier, not break up people who'd chosen each other.

"I know, I know," Grace said with a small chuckle. "I just can't help my curiosity."

"Well, I wish someone would've told me that my ex and I weren't meant for each other. Then I could've left him sooner," Iris said. "Talk about a loser."

"A bigger loser than a husband who cheats and steals your career?" Grace asked, referring to her ex-husband. He'd had an affair with the receptionist at their real estate office and then divorced Grace and locked her out of the agency she'd spent twenty years running.

Iris cleared her throat. "I'm sorry, but I think I might win the loser-husband war. He not only got involved in a drug dealing operation, but he also cost me my mayorship."

"Yeah, she might be the winner of this depressing rendition of who has the worst ex," I said, not without sympathy. "But either way, rest assured you've both chosen well the second time around."

Grace beamed. "Was that so hard?"

I snorted and led the other two women outside onto Main Street, only to come up short when Celia, a familiar ghost with big Kewpie doll eyes, appeared right in front of me.

"Help me," the waif-like ghost whispered as she blocked my path on the sidewalk.

"Celia." I sighed. I thought I'd left her behind in LA, but a few months ago, she'd appeared unexpectedly and continued to do so frequently. "What do you want now?"

"Now, you listen to me, Marion Matched. You know exactly what I want." She pumped her hips, gyrating right there in the middle of the town square. "I want a job. You need to hire me. My only compensation would be for you to find me a man. Do you know how much it sucks to be a ghost with zero prospects?"

I turned my back to her, jerking my thumb over my shoulder and asking my friends, "Do you two see this?"

"Yep," Grace said. "I'm not sure how the residents are going to feel about her mooning downtown Premonition Pointe, though."

I glanced over my shoulder, not at all surprised to find the ghost had indeed bared her backside. Rolling my eyes, I said nothing, knowing any acknowledgment from me would only encourage her.

Iris coughed and averted her eyes. "This is certainly going to make the next town meeting exciting." Her expression morphed into disbelief. "Does she always behave this way?"

"Yes. It's her way of trying to pressure me into giving her a job. She figures if she keeps embarrassing me, I'll finally cave." Turning to see why my friend's eyebrows had suddenly shot nearly to her hairline, I bit back a laugh when I spotted Celia straddling a bike rack and riding it like she was practicing for a mechanical bull.

"Gotta keep my skills fresh," the ghost said with a wink and brushed her long blond hair over one shoulder.

"Somehow, I very much doubt you've forgotten the basics," I said dryly before returning my attention back to my friends. "There was a tragic accident when she was on her way to interview with me at my old agency. The job was for a receptionist, but she wants to be in on the matchmaking even though she has no experience in the industry."

"If I can't have a love of my own," Celia insisted, "you can at least let me live vicariously."

"Do you know any dead guys looking for a date?" Grace asked, humor dancing in her bright blue eyes.

Shaking my head, I said, "I had a decent list of guys looking for a love match down in LA. However, sadly for Celia, none of them have crossed over yet. Besides, matching ghosts isn't in my current business model."

"I can fix that," Celia called. "All I need is for a tree to drop on someone. The moment I find someone with eight-pack abs, a chiseled jaw, and manly equipment worthy of me expending that kind of energy, I could make it happen. Personality doesn't matter much. I'm not in it for the conversation."

"Celia!" I admonished. "You of all... *beings*, know that words matter. Don't ever even joke about taking someone's life. Just putting that intention out there is dangerous."

Celia rolled her large eyes. "Good goddess. No one can even take a joke anymore. Fine." She waved an unconcerned hand. "Either hire me or find me someone hot to bone. That would at least get me out of your hair for a week or two."

"Just a week or two?" Grace asked, her eyes wide. Then she

narrowed them and eyed Celia shrewdly. "Seems like that's not much incentive for Marion to work on your problem."

"Fine. A month. But make sure he's hot." She smirked and then disappeared into thin air.

I blew out a relieved breath that she was gone, if only temporarily. Dealing with Celia was always a chore. I'd hoped that when I moved to Premonition Pointe I'd finally be free of the ghost, but no such luck. So here I was, trying to open a new dating service, and for some reason the universe was punishing me with a demanding ghost who had zero filters.

Grace chuckled to herself. "She's a handful."

"You can say that again," Iris agreed, her forehead wrinkling as she frowned. "Is she going to be showing up at the office regularly?"

I winced. "Probably."

"Maybe you should hire her?" Iris took out her phone and started to tap away, presumably making notes for herself. "I'm willing to bet most clients will find her entertaining. Maybe if she feels useful, she'll stop being so inappropriate."

"I wonder if that would really work," I said. "I wouldn't be opposed to hiring her. It's not like a ghost will actually cost me any dollars. The problem would be if she turns off any customers. I had a reputation of being the best down in LA. I have every intention of repeating that experience here."

I frowned, deep in thought. Premonition Pointe wasn't Los Angeles. And I was taking my business in a different direction. Instead of matching overpaid Hollywood execs with women half their age, I wanted to focus on women my own age and the men who wanted them. I was well aware I'd have to prove myself in order to build the type of reputation and volume of business I had enjoyed in my former town. Celia was going to be a problem if she was always butting in and demanding a sex buddy. But she had told me multiple times she'd clean up her act if I just gave her a job to do. Maybe that would work. I didn't particularly care to be blackmailed into anything, but if this would keep her in line, maybe it was worth it.

"Hmm, that gives me an idea," Iris said, scrolling through her phone.

I eyed her with curiosity. "You're not planning on using Celia in the marketing blitz for my grand opening, are you?"

Iris laughed. "Hardly. You said you had a reputation for being the best, right?"

"Yes," I said, my tone suspicious. "You're not going to make me find a match for the town curmudgeon, are you?"

Iris smirked. "That would really be something. But no, I have a better idea. What do you think about taking on a famous online social influencer witch who often posts about her hilarious and cringeworthy dating antics?" Iris was really getting excited now. "This is exactly the scenario that's going to launch the Miss Matched Midlife Dating Agency into the stratosphere. If she agrees, we'll take her on as a client and have her document her journey."

"Wait," I said, waving my hands. "That sounds kinda risky. What if it all goes south? It's not like we can just take back those online posts. And who wants to have their dating life on the internet for public consumption?"

Iris gave me a patient smile. "Did you miss the part about her already posting about her dating life? It's part of her brand. And do you really think it will turn out bad? Don't you have darn near a one hundred percent success rate? Come on, Marion. Have some confidence in yourself and your business. This could be gold."

She wasn't wrong. There was a reason I had a reputation for being the best in the business. Excitement started to build deep in my belly. "You're a genius, you know that? Do you really think you can get her on board?"

"I bet she can," Grace said, nodding as if she had all the confidence in the world that Iris could pull off anything.

"Thanks, Grace." Iris reached over and gave her friend a one-armed hug. She smiled at me. "Just leave it to me."

While the two brainstormed ideas to entice the social media influencer, I turned and stared at the building that was the home of my new dating agency. It was a two-story brick building with a balcony that overlooked the town square and the Pacific Ocean. In the distance, I could hear the waves crashing against the Northern California shore.

Deep in my soul, I knew I'd made the right choice moving to Premonition Pointe. The place had just called to me. However, I couldn't deny that I was nervous about opening a midlife dating agency. If it wasn't successful, I'd be back in LA within the year. And I really didn't want to give up my new home or the coven of witches who were my new ride-or-die friends.

"What do you think, Marion?" Iris asked. "Can I offer her three free months of service in exchange for her dating stories?"

I spun around, determination taking up residence in my gut. I didn't care if she ended up being the most difficult client on the planet. I'd find her a love match and change her life in the process. Just as I'd done for dozens of clients before. "Do it. Let's get started right away."

Iris nodded. "I'm on it. With any luck, we'll have her on board before the launch party mixer next week."

It'd been a few weeks since we'd started getting the business in order, and I was itching to get to work. "Perfect. In the meantime, I'll work on finding potential matches for our media star."

Celia popped back into existence and purred, "Ohhh, I just ran into the sexiest grumpy chef a few minutes ago. I bet I could tame him with just a little tickle to his ba—"

"Nope!" Grace said, laughing as she held her hand up. "That's more than I need to hear."

"Wait," Iris interjected. "I might need to hear about this tickling trick. Just last night Kade was ranting about some shipment that was held up in customs for weeks, putting him and Lucas behind on a custom order, and I really could use a new trick to get him out of his head when he gets wound up."

"It's not *this* head you need to be worried about," Celia said, pointing at her temple.

My friends started chuckling, and then when Celia went on to explain in explicit detail her tricks for calming a man, they fell out completely, laughing so hard that tears were streaming down their faces.

"Now all I can picture is Celia groping a grumpy chef while he bastes a roast, and it's just a little more than I can take." I said. "Iris, let me know after you've secured our media star, and I'll set up a meeting. Grace, thanks for everything."

"Will do," Grace forced out through her laughter.

"Perfect. Now, are you guys ready for lunch?"

Grace wiped at her eyes as she gasped for air, still trying to calm herself. "Lunch. Yes."

"Lunch?" Celia asked. "Why can't you meet for drinks at *Abs, Buns, & Guns*? I mean, nothing's better than seeing hotties shake it in hot pants while slathered in baby oil."

"She has a point, Marion," Grace said with a snicker. "Ever since that new show opened up, I've been wondering if it's as good as the *Thunder from Down Under*."

8

"Grace," I said with an exasperated sigh. "Seriously?" Then I turned to Celia. "If I give you a job, will you tone the sexual innuendo down to a bare minimum?"

The ghost's big eyes went wider than I thought possible, and she quickly nodded. "You're serious? You'll let me help you with the matchmaking? You know I'm good at knowing things, right? I can see things others can't."

"No spying!" I ordered. "If I hear of one incident of you invading anyone's privacy, I'll call someone to do a ghost cleansing so fast you'll end up like that chick in *The Exorcist* with your head spinning."

Celia scoffed, looking offended. "That's not what I meant. Please. I may be crass, but I'm not a perv. I meant I have a sixth sense for this stuff. Sort of like you do, only I don't see auras. I just know things."

Sure she did. "You mean like a gut feeling?"

"Something like that." She shrugged. "I can't really explain it."

"Okay," I relented. "Just remember that this is my reputation on the line. No mooning the town, no making lewd hip gyrations, or simulating any sexual act for attention or blackmail purposes. Got it?"

"Got it." She stood up straight, her shoulders back, and saluted me. "When do I start matching people?"

I bit back a grimace, already regretting my decision. But I powered on, knowing I was stuck with her for the foreseeable future. "Since you won't be a great fit for the office work, I'll need you at the mixer. Your job will be to keep people mingling and observe how people are getting along and then report back to me. Can you handle that?"

"Absolutely. You may not realize this, but I'm a people person. You won't be disappointed." She grinned and started to walk away from us toward the beach before she turned back, "Don't forget my compensation."

"I won't," I said, holding back a sigh. "As soon as I figure out where to find eligible bachelor ghosts, I'll see about matching you with someone." Not that I had any idea how to do that, but I'd try. Hey, maybe that could be a side business. How they'd pay was a challenge, but I was open to possibilities.

Celia's cocky expression vanished as her features softened. Her eyes met mine and I was rewarded with a soft, "Thanks, Marion. You don't know what this means to me."

I watched as she disappeared into the thin air, and wondered what had just happened. That was a side of Celia I'd never witnessed before.

Grace pressed her hand to her heart. "Wow. Who knew Celia had a sensitive side? That was a really touching moment."

I glanced at my two friends. "Do you think we'll see more of that from her?"

They both chuckled and Iris shook her head. "I wouldn't count on it."

"Yeah, me neither. Wish me luck."

"Good luck," Grace said. "You're gonna need it."

CHAPTER 2

"*Marion?*" I heard his voice right before the squeak of my screen door filled the room.

I jerked my head up from my desk and spotted my father standing in my entryway holding a suitcase. "Dad?" I jumped up and rushed over to him. "What are you doing here?"

"You invited me, didn't you?" He put his luggage down and held out his arms, waiting for a hug.

There was no hesitation as I walked into his arms and held on as he swept me up into a bear hug. Laughing, I finally stepped back and eyed him with suspicion. "Seriously, what changed your mind? I thought you were staying with Aunt Lucy." I'd been trying to get him to come visit me in Premonition Pointe ever since I'd moved to the seaside town. Since he was retired, there was nothing pressing keeping him in LA. But he'd always declined my offer when he visited and said Aunt Lucy needed him, though that was a lie. She'd been in the hospital recently, but had since made a full recovery and was busy playing pickle ball with her besties every day and then tearing it up at dance classes three nights a week. Judging by the videos she sent me, she'd be ready for *Dancing with the Stars* in no time.

"I was planning to, but she's back on her feet now and…" He shrugged. "Maybe I just wanted to see my daughter."

"Okaaay." I had my suspicions that he wasn't being completely honest, but it didn't matter. I was just happy to see him. "Come on. Let's get your luggage into the guest suite and you can tell me your plans."

"Guest suite?" he asked, following me out the front door of my small cottage. "This place has a guest suite?"

Chuckling, I waved a hand at the two-story garage. "There's a one-bedroom apartment over the garage. I figured you'd be more comfortable there than in Ty's room." Ty was the son of my late best friend, Trish. He'd been eighteen when she was tragically killed in a car accident, and he moved in with me shortly after. That had been four years ago. He was currently still working down in LA, but as soon as his contract ended, he'd be relocating to Premonition Pointe and living with me, at least temporarily.

"That's very convenient. I guess you won't mind if I stay awhile, then," he said casually as he took off for the apartment.

"A while?" I asked, running to catch up with him. "What does that mean?"

"Exactly what I said. You don't mind, do you?"

"No." I led the way up the stairs and unlocked the door for my dad. "I was just wondering how long I'm going to get to enjoy your company."

He snorted. "You're wondering when I'm going to be out of your hair."

I gave him a flat stare and then narrowed my eyes. "You know that isn't true."

"If you say so." He dropped his bags. "I'm going to unpack,

and then what do you say I take my favorite daughter out to dinner?"

"I'm your only daughter, Dad."

He winked. "As far as you know."

All I could do was shake my head at his teasing tone. "That's not as funny as you think. But sure, I'd love to go to dinner."

"Good. Give me an hour to get settled, and then I'll be ready."

His tone was clear. I'd been dismissed, and whatever answers I was looking for as to why he'd shown up on my doorstep with no firm departure date would have to wait. "Sounds good. I'll see you in a bit."

My phone was ringing when I stepped back into the house. I hurried to pick it up where I'd left it on the counter and saw it was a number I didn't recognize. I gave out my card often, so it wasn't unusual for new clients to call. I hit Accept and said, "Marion Matched. What can I do for you today?"

"You can tell that coward father of yours that I left his shit on the curb," a woman yelled over the connection.

"Candy?" I asked, frowning in confusion, hoping I'd gotten her name right. As far as I knew, Candy was the only woman my father had been dating recently.

"He left me a breakup note. A fucking note! Who does that?"

It was definitely Candy. I had only met her once just before I'd moved up to Premonition Pointe, and that had been by accident. I'd stopped by my dad's house and had run into the other woman during her walk of shame. How serious had they been if Candy was calling me about the way Dad had handled things? "Uh... I'm not sure I'm the one you should be talking to about this. Did you try calling him?"

"Memphis has been sending my calls straight to voice mail

13

since yesterday. Honestly, I don't even want to talk to his ugly ass. Just tell him if he wants his shit back, it's sitting on the curb. If he doesn't come and get it by tonight, I'm throwing it in the trash."

"Okay. I'll let him know," I said, but I quickly realized the line was already dead. Shoving my phone into my pocket, I walked out of the house and headed to the garage apartment. The front door was open and after I knocked on the door jamb, I peered through the screen door.

"Marion?" My dad blinked at me from his spot on the couch. "Has it been an hour already?"

I slipped inside, shaking my head. "Nope. But I thought you'd like to know that Candy called me."

He let out a groan. "What did she want?"

"She said she was leaving all the stuff you left behind outside on the curb and that if you didn't pick it up right away, she was trashing it."

"Of course she did." He rolled his eyes. "I don't need that extra toothbrush or the sweatpants that were probably mixed in with her laundry. I think I'll be fine. I can't believe she called you over a few trivial things."

"I imagine she wanted to yell at someone since you've gone into no-contact mode without so much as a conversation." I didn't bother to hide my judgment. As a matchmaker, I was very much on the side of communication and honesty. "You could've at least told her in person that you were ready to move on."

"Don't be mad, Marionberry," he said mildly. "If you had any idea of the shit she's pulled in the last couple of weeks, you'd be wondering why I didn't leave sooner."

"What did she do? Expect you to call when you said you

would?" The judgmental words just slipped out of my mouth before my brain caught up with my loose lips.

My father pressed his lips together and blankly stared past me as he completely shut down. Ever since my mother walked out on him over twenty years ago, my father had been a dating nightmare. He always chose women who were completely wrong for him. They'd burn red hot for a month or two and then ultimately, they'd flame out when they realized they had nothing in common. Or worse, if the woman wanted true commitment. Dad had sworn to never get married again, and at the rate he was going, I was certain he'd keep that promise. And when a woman wanted more from him, his first instinct was to ghost them.

"Sorry," I muttered. "It's none of my business."

"That's right. It's not," he warned, his tone low and even. It was the one he'd used when I was a kid that meant I was in trouble. Back then, I'd do everything I could to get back into his good graces. Now, I mostly just ignored it.

"Ready for dinner?"

"Are you going to stop berating me about my dating choices?" he shot back.

"Probably not," I said with a half smile. "If it's not me or Aunt Lucy challenging you, then who will?"

He snorted and then shook his head with a hint of amusement. "Let's go. I've been craving a burger all day."

I slipped my arm through his. "Perfect. I know just the place."

CHAPTER 3

"I have good news and bad news," Iris said the minute she walked into my office. The former mayor was dressed in slim navy pants and a matching suit jacket with a crisp white shirt underneath. Her long blond hair was swept up into a neat bun. All she needed was a pair of cat's-eye glasses to complete a hot librarian look.

I clicked out of the list I'd been working on for the mixer and gave her my full attention. "Good news first."

"I got the influencer to agree to be a client for three months," she said, biting her lower lip. It was a nervous tick that was unusual for Iris.

I leaned back in my chair and clasped my fingers behind my head. "Let me guess; the bad news is that she agreed but named an outrageous fee?"

"Yes." Iris wasn't one to mince words. She passed me the contract that we'd already written up. It was signed by the internet personality, but the woman had handwritten an extra clause about compensation.

That wasn't a surprise. I was used to working with celebrities.

"I'm sure we can find someone else," Iris said, clearly having already dismissed the idea. "Maybe we should pursue the town curmudgeon idea. People would love a good grumpy-guy-finds-love story."

"Hold that thought," I said, picking up my phone and dialing the number on the contract.

"Lennon Love," the woman said when she answered.

I held back a snicker, thinking how perfect it was that her last name was Love. "Hello, Ms. Love. This is Marion Matched of the Miss Matched Midlife Dating Agency."

"Hello, Miss Matched. I'm intrigued by your proposal to try your dating services. Does your phone call mean we've reached a deal?"

No wonder her star had risen as an online social media personality. It was immediately clear that charm and business sense was oozing from her. "I'm hoping that will be the case by the time we're done negotiating."

"Negotiating?" Lennon repeated, still sounding friendly, but there was the tiniest hint of caution. No doubt she was bombarded with offers that never paid her in actual cash. "I'm open to that, but keep in mind I know my worth."

"That's good," I said, grinning. "There's nothing better than working with a professional. Listen, I'm a straight shooter when it comes to building business relationships. I completely understand your fee, and after checking out your platform I'm certain you're worth every cent. But I was wondering if you'd be open to reducing that fee if I could get you an introduction to Tandy Knight."

There was a long pause on the other end of the line, and it was then I knew I'd struck a nerve.

"Tandy Knight?" she finally asked. "The creator of *Witch Upon a Star*, *Small Town Spells*, and *The Wicked West*?"

"That's the one," I said. "As I'm sure you know, she has a massive deal with ParaStream. I happen to know that she's currently working on a new show that's all about witches who are breakout social media stars, and I'm sure she'd love to meet you."

Lennon cleared her throat. "That sounds like something I'd be interested in, but how do I know that I'm going to get a real meeting and not just an invitation to some Hollywood party that Tandy may or may not attend?"

I nearly chuckled. This one had seen more than her share of fuckery in Hollywood. "That does happen a lot, doesn't it?"

"All the time. And excuse me for being blunt, Miss Matched, but I don't work for free or for empty promises."

"I love a girl who knows her value," I said. "Don't worry. I'm not looking for free work. I'm only looking for a reduced rate in exchange for a formal meeting with Tandy."

There was another long pause. "How is it exactly that you can promise meetings with Tandy Knight?"

"Now that's confidential," I said, unwilling to disclose that I'd matched Tandy with the love of her life a few years earlier. It hadn't been easy, and had I not been tenacious, those two would still be passing each other like ships in the night. Tandy had been so grateful she'd invited me over for a private dinner, and after that, we'd become the best of friends. The kind of friends who text every day. And Tandy had already expressed an interest in meeting the influencer when I'd mentioned Iris's plan to her. "But I am willing to put in a clause stipulating that if the meeting doesn't happen within ninety days of the signed contract, that I'll pay your regular fee."

"Seriously?" Lennon said, sounding stunned.

"Seriously. Do we have a deal?"

"Yes." There wasn't even the slightest hint of hesitation, which was remarkable since I hadn't even told her what the reduced rate would be. But I knew a meeting with the hottest producer on the hottest new streaming network would be too juicy to pass up.

"Excellent. I'll have my business manager call you shortly to arrange the final details. And Lennon?"

"Yeah?"

"I look forward to meeting you."

"You, too," she said, sounding a little in awe of how the conversation had gone.

After I ended the call, I turned to Iris. "Looks like the problem is solved. Can you give her a call back to take care of the contract changes?"

"Of course." She jotted down a note. "How much is a meeting with Tandy worth?"

"Probably more than her entire fee. Especially if that meeting goes the way I think it will. Offer her fifty percent of her rate. If she negotiates, go as high as sixty."

"You got it." Iris shook her head and chuckled softly. "I have no idea why you hired me. You've clearly got this handled."

I side-eyed her. "Come on now, Iris. Don't act like I could do all of this by myself. You know I need you."

"Maybe for paperwork," she conceded. "But a woman who has Tandy Knight on speed dial probably has better contacts than a former small-town mayor."

"You know everyone in town and worked your ass off to get my business up and running in less than six months. Trust me, you're the right woman for the job."

"Well, that's good because you're stuck with me for the

foreseeable future," Iris finally said with a smile and then retreated to her desk to make that phone call.

An hour later, with the contract signed and filed, Iris stood at my desk and said, "Come on. I'm taking you to lunch before you forget again."

"I can't say no to that. What did you have in mind?"

"How do you feel about crab melts?" she asked, already leading the way out of the office.

"Love them."

"Perfect. I know just the place." Iris swept out of the office, never once turning to be sure I was following her.

Chuckling, I grabbed my keys, locked up, and joined her out front on the sidewalk. It was mid-January, but it was a glorious sunny day. It was rare, but Premonition Pointe did sometimes have warm days during January and February. It was one of the things I loved about the town. I turned my face to the sun, smiling at the warmth on my skin and said, "Okay. Where to?"

"See that food truck over there?" She pointed across the square to a silver truck that was parked in a parking lot that overlooked the Pacific Ocean.

"You're taking me to a food truck?" I asked with a light chuckle.

"Not just any food truck. The best damned food truck in the state."

"In the entire state?" I asked, amused. "Who decided the list?"

"I did. Now come on before the line is a mile long."

Sure enough, when we reached the truck, the line was starting to curl around the parking lot.

"Iris, Marion!" Grace Valentine called from a picnic table near the water. "Isn't today glorious?"

We walked over to her table, both of us nodding.

When she stood, I gave her a quick hug. So did Iris, but Iris quickly said her hellos and excused herself to go stand in line. I started to follow her, but she waved me off, indicating that I should stay with Grace. "No point in both of us waiting for our turn," she said. "I've got it. You keep Grace company."

"I'll get lunch next time," I assured her and then took a seat across from Grace and asked, "No house showings today?"

"I have one this afternoon. It's haunted, too, so that should be interesting. Hopefully the buyer isn't the nervous type. I just came from a closing and stopped to get something to eat. Just in time, too. If I'd been five minutes later, I'd be at the back of the line with Iris. I can't believe how popular the truck has gotten in just a week."

"Premonition Pointe is a small town. Nothing stays secret for long," I said.

Grace glanced over my shoulder and raised one eyebrow. "That's what I thought, too, but now I'm starting to question that assumption."

What did that mean? I frowned at her and then glanced over my shoulder. My eyes widened when I spotted Jax Williams, my high school sweetheart, headed straight for us.

"That's my cue," Grace said with a slight chuckle. "I think I'll go help Iris."

"Help her with what? Surely she can manage two sandwiches and a couple of drinks," I said, eyeing her with suspicion.

"I can't resist that cheesecake on a stick," she said, waving her fingers at me as she hurried to find Iris, who was still in line.

"Marion," Jax said with his easy smile. "It seems the entire town has come out to try the crab melts."

"It seems so," I said, unable to stop the butterflies taking flight in my stomach. Dammit. Why, after all these years, did he still affect me like that?

He slid onto the bench across from me and grinned.

"Why are you looking at me like that?" I asked, my eyes narrowed in suspicion.

His dark eyes lit up with amusement as he laughed. "Still the same Marion. It's nice to know that some things don't ever really change."

Some things did. Like the fact that when I was eighteen years old, I was certain that Jax was my future. But then he'd gone off to college, and it had been too hard to stay together. Not to mention that I'd always known our relationship wasn't meant to be. My gift of matchmaking was also my curse. I could always tell when people were a good match for each other by reading their auras. When two people were together who were meant to be, their auras turned a deep violet color. Their energies also had a feeling of what I referred to as rightness. They just felt settled. At ease. It was as if the universe had spoken.

When Jax and I were together, his aura was deep red. There'd always been passion between us, an intensity that went bone deep. But that violet, all-is-right-with-the-world aura had never appeared. When I'd been younger, I'd thought that passion was enough to carry a relationship. Now that I'd lived a full life, I knew for certain it wasn't. And more than anything, I wanted Jax to live a happy, joyful life. Not one that was always on the verge of imploding due to a tumultuous relationship.

I'd witnessed that deep violet aura when he'd been with his ex-wife. I had no idea what had happened between them, but I had no doubt that they'd had many good years together. It sometimes happened like that. Two people were perfect for each other, but then something changes and the relationship no longer works. Time could be a difficult mistress as people live their lives and evolve. Forever wasn't always forever, as much as I wished that could be the case. Still, whatever the reason for their divorce, Jax deserved to have that type of love again, and it wouldn't be with me.

I cleared my throat and finally answered him. "What do you mean, some things never change?"

"You. I swear you barely look a day over eighteen years old." He winked and flashed me his killer smile, the one that made that dimple on his right cheek appear.

Holy hell. Could the man get any more devastating? Trying to hide the fact that I found him completely charming, I rolled my eyes. "Please. The crow's feet around my eyes tell a completely different story."

He squinted as if trying to make them out. Then he shook his head. "Nope. Must just be your imagination. All I see is a gorgeous woman who couldn't possibly have been in my graduating class."

"You should make an appointment with your optometrist," I deadpanned. "Either you need some serious eye correction, or you're being an incorrigible flirt."

"It's probably both." His shoulders were relaxed, but his normally pale-yellow aura was turning orange, and I knew from experience the longer we talked, the darker it would get until his energy turned completely red.

I nearly sighed with the realization that there would probably never be a day when we weren't attracted to each other. No doubt, if I could see my own aura, it'd be cherry red already. I wanted this man. I'd always wanted him. When I closed my eyes at night, he was the one who popped into my mind. Even after all these years, I could still feel his touch, his lips, his body hovering over mine as he had so many times that summer after we'd graduated. Our bodies just called to each other. They always had.

Jax eyed me thoughtfully. Then he said, "Go out with me tonight."

His invitation caught me off guard, and I just blinked at him for a second.

He chuckled. "I love that I still have that effect on you."

"Humble much?" I asked, my tone void of any judgment as I smiled at him. How could I not? The man just got under my skin in a way no one else ever had.

"Just honest. What do you say? A walk on the beach at sunset and some dinner? There's that new farm-to-table restaurant in town."

I wanted so badly to say yes. I was single. He was single. Just because we weren't each other's soul mates didn't mean we couldn't spend time together. I had almost convinced myself to accept when a tall blonde walked over to our table and placed a hand on Jax's shoulder.

"Hey, Jax." She smiled down at him, her aura quickly turning a deep shade of violet.

He placed his hand over hers and returned the smile as his aura shifted from a red hue to light blue. "Bethany. I didn't know you were back in town already."

"I just got back a few hours ago." She squeezed his hand. "Thanks for checking in on Boots for me while I was away. I'm guessing you spent some quality time with him, too, since he hasn't tried to scratch my eyes out for being gone for days."

"I might have sat on the couch and watched *Yellowstone* with him a few nights," Jax said, his dimple flashing at her.

My stomach churned with unease as his aura quickly

melded into that deep violet color. There was no question the two were perfect for each other. If I was a better woman, I'd have suggested Jax take Bethany to the new farm-to-table restaurant. Instead, I sat there silently, knowing that the only man I'd ever wanted was destined for the gorgeous blonde.

"I'll come by later for that drink you owe me," Jax said, finally dropping her hand.

"You do that." She bent down and kissed his cheek, and when she straightened, she glanced at me, looking almost startled. "I'm sorry. How rude of me." She held her hand out. "I'm Bethany Olsen, Jax's neighbor."

"Hi, Bethany," I said politely. "I'm Marion Matched. Jax and I went to high school together."

"Marion Matched?" she asked, her eyes lighting with excitement. "The matchmaker, right?"

"That's me," I said, giving her my full attention when Celia appeared out of nowhere.

"Oh, this is interesting," the ghost said, gleefully rubbing her hands together. "My first assignment. You two look like you could use a little help in the matchmaking department."

"You think?" Bethany asked, her eyes lighting up as she looked at Jax.

Jax looked like a deer caught in the headlights.

I cleared my throat. "Celia, we don't make matches unless and until people ask us to. You understand that, right?"

Celia rolled her eyes and placed her hands on her torso as she pushed up her breasts, showing off her assets for no apparent reason. "Of course I do, but it's hard keeping all this talent to myself."

Both Jax and Bethany turned to stare at the ghost. Bethany tilted her head to the side, studying her. "Do I know you from somewhere?"

Celia preened and flicked her long blond hair over one shoulder. "You probably recognize me from my time on television."

It was all I could do to keep my snort of laughter in.

Bethany's eyes lit up. "That's it. You were on that sitcom about the rich family who loses everything and inherits a motel in some small city. Something Creek, right? I just love that father and son duo. Seriously, the best show on television."

Celia's smile turned plastic as she shrugged one shoulder and said, "My role was pretty small, so I didn't spend much time with the principle actors."

More like zero time. Celia wasn't on that hit show. She hadn't been on any show, though she'd certainly auditioned for plenty.

"That's too bad," Bethany said. "But still, that must have been the experience of a lifetime."

Before she could answer, Jax chimed in. "Weren't you the face of Unicorn Lube?"

Bethany blinked.

Celia's face turned bright red, and I had a moment of wonder at how a ghost managed to blush. "It was an entry-level gig."

"Sure," Jax said seriously. "You must have practiced a lot to get that wrist action down to a science. It's not everyone who can slick a dildo with sparkly lube with such perfection." He gave her a sly grin. "I heard their sales tripled after your commercial aired. Men everywhere wanted to see their dicks sparkle."

I couldn't help it; a laugh burst from my lips and a moment later, I gasped, trying to get air in my lungs as I laughed so hard my sides started to hurt.

Jax chuckled along with me while Bethany looked slightly

confused and asked, "Unicorn Lube? Are you saying someone sells lube that actually sparkles? And men are purchasing it?"

"Of course they are," Celia said haughtily. "If they think they can get someone as hot as me, they'll put anything on their junk."

Her comment only made me laugh harder until tears ran down my cheeks.

Celia huffed and said, "Bite me." The ghost rose from her place at the table and followed a man half-dressed in a wetsuit as he made his way down to the beach with a surfboard.

I mentally prayed she didn't try to drown him just so she could get a date.

"Oh. Well, whatever works." Bethany turned to Jax. "Are you going to Marion's mixer Friday night?"

"I hadn't really—" Jax started.

"He is," I interjected, seeing the perfect opportunity to set them up, even though I'd just told Celia we only did that for paying clients. There was just no denying that they would be a great match. My heart ached at the thought, but it was for the best.

He raised one eyebrow as he stared at me. "I am?"

"You are," I said, lifting my chin slightly. "You're going to support the launch of an old friend's new business."

He held my gaze for a long moment before nodding and turning to Bethany. "It looks like I'll be there."

"Great." She leaned over and gave him another kiss on the cheek. "Maybe we can go together."

"Maybe. I'll need to check and see what my schedule looks like that day," he said, sounding more than a little hesitant.

"Perfect. Just text me," Bethany said, sounding pleased with herself. Turning to me, she said. "I was always planning to go to your party, but now I'm looking forward to it." She winked at Jax and then waggled her fingers as she sauntered over to the food truck line.

"I'm not going to date her," Jax said as soon as she was out of earshot.

"Why not?" I asked pointedly. "She's perfect for you. You should take her to dinner tonight."

"Does that mean I'm still available?"

I nodded, knowing it was the right thing to do.

"Then it's leftovers for me, I guess. She reminds me too much of my ex-wife." He reached across the table and took my hand in his. Using his thumb, he caressed the back of my hand as he added, "Besides, I have my eye on someone else."

"Jax," I started.

But before I could find the words to discourage him, he rose to his feet and said, "You can fight it all you want, but someday, Marion Matched, you're going to realize that auras don't always have all the answers. You were always meant to be mine. I know it, and you know it too. I think maybe you're just a little too scared to admit it."

I stared at him, my heart beating rapidly as he walked off and disappeared behind the crowd still waiting in line for their lunch.

"Whoa," Iris said.

I glanced up to find my business manager fanning herself. She'd placed two paper plates on the table and was grinning ear to ear. "If that wasn't a line made for a romance novel, then I don't know what is."

I groaned, looked at the crab melts that were swimming in cheese, and groaned again. That for sure wasn't going to help me lose the extra twenty pounds I was carrying. But at that moment, there was no going back. I grabbed one of the plates, turned off the guilt trying to take over my mind, and took a mouth-watering bite. I'd start my diet tomorrow.

CHAPTER 4

I sat out on the front porch, sipping a glass of iced
tea as I went over the details for the mixer the
following night. It had been a good week. I'd lined up half a
dozen new clients who would be at the mixer to meet the
influencer. If all went well, I'd end up with a few solid matches
for her. And maybe one for Jax. It wasn't unusual for me to hit
the matches out of the park on the first pairing, but it wasn't a
given either.

Jax had been right about one thing; auras didn't always tell
the entire story. Two people's auras could be the deepest violet,
but they could still have deal-breaker issues that kept them
apart. Things like kids or no kids was a huge one. Religion
could sometimes play a role. Then there were other issues like
the woman who was determined to spend her life traveling as
much as possible and the man I'd matched her with who never
wanted to leave their small town just outside of Santa Barbara.
They needed to agree on the basics before they could commit
to a life together.

I ran my finger around the rim of my glass, trying not to

think about the way Jax had looked at me. There'd been hunger there, but it wasn't as if he'd been channeling that he wanted to take me home and rip my clothes off. That was something I could deal with. But no, he'd been looking at me like he wanted to take me home and move me right in. Like he wanted me all to himself on every level, not just a physical one.

Dammit if I didn't want that, too, but what would happen when the fire burned out. Jax was too important to me. He'd always been the one who got away. And honestly, I liked it that way. The hope of a future with someone I really cared about was always there, just out of reach but never impossible. If I gave in, and we gave this thing between us a chance and it didn't work out, I wouldn't even have that. Then I'd have to face the possibility that I'd never get my happily-ever-after.

"Marion!" a woman called.

I glanced up and spotted Tazia Bellini, a woman closer to my dad's age than my own, strolling up my walkway to the porch. Her auburn hair was pulled up into a messy bun, and she was wearing a loose-fitting sundress. Her look, combined with the bundle of sunflowers she was holding in her right hand, made her appear as if she'd walked right out of the late sixties.

"Tazia." I stood and walked down the steps to greet her. "You're back. How was the trip to New England?"

"Good. I got to see my grandbabies and then met up with an old friend. We went into the city and watched a couple of Broadway shows. I froze my tatas off, but it was worth it." She handed me the bundle of sunflowers. "These are for you from my greenhouse."

"Thank you." I took the flowers and gave her a hug. Tazia lived a few streets over. I'd met her one evening on a walk shortly after I'd moved in, and we'd become fast friends. Her passion was gardening, and she spent most of her time outdoors or in her greenhouse. She was forever bringing me bundles of flowers, which only made me love her more.

"Come on up to the porch and have a glass of wine with me," I said, waving for her to follow me.

"That sounds wonderful."

I left her in one of my chairs on the porch as I went in to put the flowers in water and pour her a glass of wine. When I returned, I heard my father's deep chuckle. The pair were sitting side by side, their heads together as they stared at something on Tazia's phone.

"Hey, Dad," I said as I handed Tazia her glass of wine. "Want something to drink?"

He eyed Tazia's glass for a moment but then shook his head. "No. I better not. I'm headed off to a poker game down at the Pelican. I'd like to be clear-headed for at least the first few hands." He stood and shoved his hands in his pockets. "It was nice meeting you, Tazia."

"You, too, Memphis." Tazia smiled softly at him, and just like that, her aura shifted to meld with my father's. They'd both been bathed in light blue, but when they looked at each other, their auras darkened and it was almost as if the world had stopped turning. Magic was in the air, crackling over my skin, and I knew without a doubt that Tazia and my father were meant to be together. Joy skittered straight to my heart. Tazia was fantastic. She was just the type of woman who was perfect for him—fun, independent, smart, and the kindest person I'd met in a long time.

After my father's car had disappeared around the corner, I turned to Tazia. "Are you busy tomorrow night?"

She shook her head. "What did you have in mind?"

"It's a launch party mixer thing for Miss Matched. I'd love it if you could come."

Tazia narrowed her eyes at me. "Are you trying to find me a date?"

"Nope," I said, shaking my head. I'd already found one. Now all I had to do was get both of them to agree to spending time together. "I just thought it would be nice to have a friendly face there."

Her shoulders relaxed as she sat back in the chair. "In that case, I wouldn't miss it for the world."

I stood near the front windows of Witches' Garden and surveyed the crowd. Lennon Love was standing off in a corner with Bodhi Bliss, another social media influencer I'd stumbled on when I'd been doing research on Lennon. He'd been her boyfriend and business partner some years back, right out of college. The business had failed, and with it, so had the relationship. Normally I wouldn't actively try to set up one of my clients with a former love interest, but since the internet was a sucker for second-chance romances, I'd taken the chance.

Surprisingly, the two were not only rocking violet auras when they were together, but they also couldn't keep their eyes off each other. There was no doubt about it. Bodhi was the one for Lennon.

I smiled to myself. This was going to be a major hit on social media.

The place was starting to fill up, so I made my rounds, spotting Bethany chatting with a local artist. He showed his paintings at a local gallery. While they seemed to be having a good time, their auras said they weren't a match. My heart sank a little, and it was then I realized that I was hoping to find her someone so that I didn't have to set her up with Jax.

"Snap out of it, Marion," I whispered to myself and continued to weave my way through my guests. After spotting my dad holding court at a table in the back, I wasn't surprised to see that none of the ladies at his table were right for him. Their auras were a clash of colors, indicating that dating would be a disaster. But if history were to repeat itself, no doubt he'd date at least three of them for a few weeks before the superficial relationships flamed out.

"Okay, boss, I'm here," Celia said, popping into the restaurant from thin air. "What do you want me to do?"

"You're late," I said dryly.

"How am I supposed to tell time?" she asked, sounding irritated. "It's not like I have a watch, or even a wall clock across from my nonexistent couch. Do you know how hard it is to track time in the afterlife?"

I blinked at her. "No."

"Thank your lucky stars. It's a bitch." She glanced around the space and grinned. "Now this is a party. You turned out the babes for that internet chick. Now if only you could do that for me."

Once again, I ignored her commentary and said, "I need you to find Tazia and get her to my dad's table. Can you handle that?"

"Yes, ma'am. I'm on it." She patted her dress as if to remove any wrinkles and then headed in the opposite direction with a bright smile on her face.

I took note of Lennon again and found her happily chatting with a group of men and women. Good. The more people she met the better.

Now where were Celia and Tazia? There they were. Celia was bobbing next to Tazia, chattering cheerfully about... Had she just mimed two people going at it? I stared at her hands, and yes, she was doing the universal signal for two people boning. I gritted my teeth and walked over to them.

"Celia? What did I say about not being inappropriate?"

The ghost gave me an innocent smile. "I was just telling Tazia a story. No need to go all *Devil Wears Prada* on me."

"I'm not—what? I don't know what that means," I said frowning.

Tazia laughed. "It just means she'd like you to relax a little."

"There's time to relax later. Right now, we need to make some love matches." I turned back to my ghost assistant. "Can you introduce Sara Groveland to a couple of other men? I already know she isn't right for my father." I gestured to his table and the petite brunette who was sitting to his left.

Tazia smirked at me. "I know what you're doing."

I gave her the most innocent look I could muster. "I have no idea what you're talking about."

"Sure you don't." Still, she followed Celia and took Sara's chair. It didn't take long for her to cover my dad's hand with hers and laugh at something he'd said.

Perfect. If the gods were with me, Tazia would charm my dad, and when I sent them on a mini date, he wouldn't balk at the idea.

I glanced at the door and then scanned the room, looking for Jax. It wasn't the first time I'd looked for him, and it wouldn't be the last. The mixer had started forty-five minutes earlier, and I was starting to wonder if he was going to show.

"Look," Iris said, appearing beside me and nudging my arm.

I followed her gaze and spotted Celia introducing Sara to a man twenty years her junior. Bain, the musician. If I wasn't mistaken, he'd just turned forty a month ago. "What in the world is Celia doing?"

"Her job?" Iris asked with a smirk.

"Seriously? She's a boomer, he's a millennial. That's a terrible match."

"Probably not in the bedroom," Iris said with a chuckle.

"Oh my gods. Celia's rubbed off on you, hasn't she?" I demanded.

Iris shook her head in amusement. "Come on, Marion. Relax a little. She's a young boomer and he's probably on the cusp of Gen X. Besides, there's nothing wrong with dating a guy with a little energy, right?"

"No, but..." I squinted at the pair. Were their auras turning violet? While I stared at them, I noticed Celia was gone, but Lennon Love joined them and suddenly sparks were flying between the musician and the influencer. My nerves calmed, and Celia's antics didn't seem to matter anymore. I'd recruited Bain specifically to introduce to Lennon. And my gut had known before I'd even seen them together. Sometimes all I had to do was stand back and wait for the magic to happen. With two really great matches, it was hard to know which she'd pick, but I knew who I was rooting for. I'd always been a sucker for a second-chance romance.

Now I just needed to find someone age-appropriate for Sara. Pleased with myself, I grabbed a champagne flute from one of the servers, but the moment I took a sip, all hell broke loose.

CHAPTER 5

"*A* penis pump!" a woman yelled, followed by, "What the hell kind of dating service takes on a client whose equipment doesn't work?"

"Penis pump?" someone else echoed in surprise. "Who uses a penis pump? The old guy with the ghost?"

My head jerked to take in a tall, white-haired man who was by the door. Celia was standing next to him, scowling at the person who'd questioned his sexual prowess. "Take that back. Sir Vincent certainly doesn't have any problems with his junk." She swept her gaze over him. "Do you?"

He gave her a slow smile and then shook his head.

Good goddess. Celia had been busy. When had she found time to find a man? I squinted at him and realized his skin looked kind of translucent. Then it hit me.

He was a ghost!

At least that explained why I hadn't recognized him. I wondered for half a second where he came from until someone else called out, "No, not him. The penis pump belongs to Memphis."

The woman who'd first blurted the words stood up from my father's table and pointed at him. Her bleach-blond hair had fallen into her eyes, and she quickly pushed it aside as she held her phone up as if everyone could see what was displayed on the small screen.

"What?" my father said, standing so fast that he knocked his chair over. "I don't even know what a penis pump is."

"Please. It's right here in full color all over your Facebook page," the bleach-blonde said, tapping her phone.

"Hold on just a minute," I said, moving toward the commotion, waving my hands as I finally snapped out of the shock that had rendered me frozen. "What exactly are you talking about?"

Blondie thrust her phone at me. "See? Penis pump and golden shower videos. Not to mention the G-strings and anal beads."

"Now *that* sounds like a good time," a smaller woman with heavy eyeliner and a loud print dress said, giving my dad a sly smile.

He visibly shuddered.

"What in the fresh hell?" I muttered as I took the phone from the woman and scrolled my dad's Facebook page. "Candy," I spit out as if her name were a curse. "She's the one who posted this crap on your page, Dad. She also tagged a bunch of people. Looks like they are all friends you both share."

"Son of a bitch!" my dad bit out. Then he took a deep breath and seemed to try to center himself.

"I don't think I can be associated with a dating service who offers up sex degenerates as their bachelors," a woman said from behind me.

When I turned around, I only caught a glimpse of a

turquoise blue skirt as a woman quickly made her way toward the front door.

I turned back and raised my arms, waving them and asking everyone to settle down, determined to put the record straight.

But before anyone noticed me, my father shouted, "Listen up everyone!" As he tried to climb onto the table in front of him, he let out a cry and fell forward when the table collapsed beneath him, knocking into the woman with the loud print dress. The one who'd thought my father would be a good time. She stumbled backward, ramming right into me, and sending us both to the ground along with the table behind us.

There was something that sounded like a mini explosion that made my ears ring, and for just a moment, I couldn't hear a thing. The woman rolled off me and scrambled to her feet, taking off through the crowd. With the wind knocked out of me, I watched in horror as the candle from the table I'd toppled over rolled and lit the table cloth on fire with a woosh!

A couple of people screamed, and suddenly everyone was quickly making their way out of the restaurant, only to be stymied at the front door as everyone tried to go through at once.

"Marion, move," my father ordered as he pulled me to my feet, took my elbow, and led me toward a side exit in the back of the restaurant.

"I have to make sure everyone gets out," I said, unable and unwilling to leave while my guests were still in the building. The fire was quickly spreading to the table my father had broken, and it occurred to me that the alcohol was probably fueling the flames. I quickly glanced around, looking for a fire extinguisher. Hadn't the manager shown me where they were when we'd done the walk-through?

There, just on the other side of the kitchen door. That's

where they always were. I made a beeline for the kitchen door, ignoring my father's demands that I leave the building. "Usher people out the side exit," I ordered.

He frowned at me but then nodded and quickly jumped into action.

The fire extinguisher was exactly where it should be. I grabbed it and pulled the pin with trembling hands, breaking the seal. Smoke started to sting my eyes when I moved close to the blaze, and my lungs started to protest. I quickly pulled my shirt up, covering my mouth, and aimed the extinguisher at the flames. Foam sprayed the area, putting out part of the fire, but it was clear I wasn't going to smother the blaze with just the one extinguisher.

The place was starting to fill with too much smoke. Tears stung my eyes, and there was no other choice but to flee the building. I turned, looking for the side exit, but quickly realized I wasn't exactly sure where I was. The smoke was too thick. Dropping to my knees, I squinted, trying to get a feel for where I was. But before I could move, a strong arm caught me by the middle and a man dressed in yellow fireman's gear hauled me up and over his shoulder.

I clung to the man, relief rushing through me even as I pleaded for him to make sure everyone else got out of the building.

"Your dad already has that handled," he said in a low, familiar voice.

Even over the sounds of the panicked crowd, I'd know that voice anywhere.

Jax Williams.

I closed my eyes and tightened my hold. As shaken as I was by the turn of events, it wasn't lost on me that the one and only person I'd ever loved had just saved me from a burning building. Talk about something right out of a romance novel. Although I knew Jax was a volunteer firefighter and was just doing his job, for a moment I let myself pretend that he'd rushed into the restaurant, intent on saving the love of his life.

A girl could dream, couldn't she?

"What in the hell did you think you were doing?" Jax demanded the moment he set me down at the back of his pickup truck.

I took a seat on the tailgate and just looked up into his handsome face, unable to even form a sentence. The shock of the fire, along with the adrenaline that had kicked in, was quickly starting to wear off and reality was setting in. Smoke was billowing out of the restaurant, and emergency lights were flashing as the vehicles pulled into the parking lot, their lights flickering in the clear night. I blinked, trying to see past the police car that had just pulled up next to us.

Dad's voice carried over the crowd, and I heard him shepherding people away from the restaurant. My nerves eased a bit, knowing he was safe.

"Marion," Jax demanded. "Did you hear what I said?"

I nodded, but instead of answering his question, I noticed the Premonition Point firetruck arriving and asked, "How did you get here so fast?"

"I was on my way here to stop by like I promised when the call came in. I didn't wait for the rest of the unit." He straightened and glanced around. "I have to go talk to the fire chief. Wait for me here."

Shaking my head, I pushed myself off the tailgate and said, "I need to check on my guests."

"You need to wait for a medic." He gently lifted me and placed me back onto his tailgate. "Smoke inhalation is nothing to mess around with. Promise me you'll stay right here while I find a paramedic."

I wasn't sure I could sit still. Not without him there to distract me. But I nodded anyway, knowing that if I refused, he'd find someone to babysit me while he took care of business.

"Promise me you'll stay here until a medic checks out your lungs," he said again, his dark eyes searching mine.

How could I say no to him? I never could. Nodding, I reached for his hand and squeezed. "Thank you for..." I swallowed hard. "Just thank you."

Jax didn't say a word. He just reached for me and pulled me into a tight hug. Pressing his lips to the top of my head, in a gruff voice he said, "I don't know what I would have done if something had happened to you."

I tilted my head back, looking up at him. So many unspoken words passed between us. Regret, longing, relief. But before I could voice anything else, he let me go and walked over to where the fire chief was waiting.

On his way, he was intercepted by Bethany. Her panicked voice carried over to me. "Oh, Jax! Thank the gods you're okay. I wasn't sure where you were, and I was so worried you were caught up in the blaze."

Blaze? I glanced at the restaurant. Firemen were rushing in. There was a lot of smoke, but the place wasn't burning to the ground. At least not yet. Her over-the-top concern grated on my nerves. He was a volunteer firefighter. Jax could handle himself in an emergency.

Jax said something to Bethany I couldn't hear and then sidestepped her to get to his fire chief.

The paramedic showed up a moment later. He went through a variety of field tests before determining that I didn't need to seek additional medical care, though he cautioned me to call my doctor immediately if I developed a cough, headache, or shortness of breath. I promised I would and then finally turned my attention to the half dozen police cruisers that were parked in front of the restaurant.

"Marion!" Iris called when she spotted me coming toward them. "Thank the gods. There you are." She crushed me into a hug. "I was so worried when we didn't see you come out of the restaurant. But the firefighters said there was no one left in the building, so we were starting to wonder if those assholes kidnapped you or something."

Furrowing my brows in confusion, I asked, "What assholes?"

"The ones that left that message on your car. You haven't seen it?"

I slowly shook my head. "No." Then I turned and spotted my white SUV that was parked under a lamppost. Nothing appeared to be out of place. Not even the Miss Matched Midlife Dating Agency decal I'd had put on it last month. Frowning, I said, "I don't see anything unusual."

Iris followed my gaze and then let out a little gasp. "Oh no. If it's not your car, then it must be Lennon's." She pointed behind me.

I turned and spotted another white, though slightly smaller, SUV with the same Miss Matched decal that had been part of the contract negotiations. The message was loud and clear.

Go back to where you came from, bitch!

CHAPTER 6

"Oh my gods!" I gasped out, my eyes wide and my gut clenched with the knowledge that one of my clients had been targeted at one of my events. "Where's Lennon?"

"Over there." Iris nodded toward the first responders gathered toward the entrance of the restaurant.

The gorgeous influencer was holding onto Jax's arm as she spoke urgently to one of the police officers. It was clear she'd already seen the message.

"I'm sorry," Iris said as she rushed along beside me. "I was so worried about you, I completely forgot we'd negotiated decals for Lennon's car, let alone the fact that she had a white SUV. I should've realized the car belonged to our high-profile client."

"No, don't worry about it," I said, hearing the exhaustion in my tone. It had been one hell of a night, and it looked to be far from over. "If I hadn't known where I was parked, I could've easily mistaken her car for mine, too. Let's just go make sure she's okay."

Iris kept pace with my brisk step and was the first one to

speak when we reached Lennon. "Lennon, are you all right? What can we do for you?"

Lennon glanced at Iris and then at me. "I'd be lying if I said this didn't shake me up, but being a public figure, this stuff does happen sometimes."

It wouldn't have taken much for someone to find out where Lennon would be that night. She'd already posted on her social media about the dating arrangement and that she'd be at a mixer tonight. She'd been vague about where it would be hosted, but Premonition Pointe was a small beach town. Renting out an entire restaurant for the evening wasn't something that went unnoticed.

"I'm so sorry this happened," I said, squeezing her hand. Turning to the policeman who was standing next to her, I said, "I'm sure the restaurant owners have security footage. Has anyone called them yet?"

"We're on it, Ms. Matched."

"It's Miss," I said automatically, even though it hardly mattered. But since it was in the name of my business, I'd found myself correcting anyone who used the other prefix.

"Right. Well, Miss Matched, we'll be pursuing every avenue in order to find the perpetrator. In the meantime, we need to ask you some questions about the incident inside the restaurant."

I cringed. "Of course."

We stepped away from Iris and Lennon and joined the fire chief. I did my best to answer their questions about how the fire had started. When I'd satisfied all their questions, they assured me that while there would be an investigation, so far it appeared the fire would be ruled a freak accident.

Freak. Sure. If only I hadn't insisted on using live candles, none of this would've happened. But no, I'd been too worried about making sure everything was romantic. How was I supposed to foresee someone like my own father climbing on the tables? It wasn't a bachelorette party for the goddess's sake. It had been a meet and greet where I observed who might be a good match so that I could set up some dates.

"Marion!" Bellatrix Malone, the owner of Witches' Garden, called as she hurried toward me. "Is everyone all right? No one was hurt, were they?"

I shook my head. "No. Everyone is fine. I can't apologize enough."

"I know, dear," the woman said, clutching my hands. "It's okay. We have insurance. As long as no one was hurt, that's the most important thing. I'm just hoping the damage isn't too severe."

"I hope so, too."

Bellatrix was pulled away to talk to the first responders, leaving me standing there gawking at the woman. If I owned a restaurant and my clients had accidentally almost burned it to the ground, I'm certain I wouldn't have been nearly that gracious. Though when she found out my father was to blame, her understanding was likely to be a thing of the past.

"I just think I should lock it down for a while," Lennon was saying when I joined her and Iris again. "Living my life so out in the open just gets me this." She waved a disgusted hand toward her car. "What happens next? They show up at my house? I've been way too open about too much, don't you think?" she asked Iris.

Iris met my gaze, her expression a little like a deer in the headlights. No doubt she wasn't sure what to say to the social influencer.

I cleared my throat and waited for Lennon to turn her attention to me. "You have to do whatever keeps you safe."

Lennon let out a sigh, looking thoroughly relieved. "I'm so glad you said that. Because I think I'm going to have to lockdown my account until whoever did this is caught. I'm just too exposed."

"She has a contract, doesn't she?" Celia said, appearing out of nowhere again.

"Celia!" I admonished. "Now isn't the time."

"I should say not," Lennon said, her tone cold.

"I was just saying people need to honor their word, that's all," Celia said, giving me a pointed look before she floated away. I wondered briefly what that was about, but quickly pushed it to the back of my mind as I turned my attention back to Lennon. Her arms were crossed over her chest, and she was scowling at us.

That was it. There went any hopes of going viral with Lennon's postings about her dating experiences with my agency. It wasn't that I blamed her. If I feared someone was targeting me, I'd do the same. But I'd spent a large portion of my marketing budget on her fee. This would not get the return on my investment that I'd hoped for.

"I'm sorry, Marion," Lennon said with finality. "I can't be the face of Miss Matched now. Not after this." Her gaze landed on her vehicle and I couldn't argue.

"I understand. Please, don't worry about it." I was disappointed, but in the end, her safety was what mattered.

"What about all your other endorsements?" Iris asked her. "I'd hate for you to forfeit your main source of income because of some asshole who is trying to scare you."

"He's not just trying. He's succeeding," she said quietly.

My heart started to ache for the other woman. "Lennon, I—"

I was about to say something supportive and make sure she

knew I was behind her, whatever she needed, but Jax appeared beside me and said, "The chief has given the all clear. Everyone is free to go for the evening. Does anyone need a ride?"

"I do," Lennon said, gazing at him with interest sparking in her bright green eyes.

Jax's gaze swept over her, and I had to hold myself back from slipping my arm around him as if I were claiming him as my own. My one saving grace was that their auras were a complete mismatch. Jax's was a calming blue, while Lennon's was a burnt orange, indicating a certain amount of stress. That was normal. But the two auras seemed to bump into each other instead of merging like they usually did when two people were a good match.

"Hi, I'm Lennon," the petite brunette said, holding her hand out to him.

He took her hand and flashed her his dimpled smile. Even though I knew Jax wasn't interested in her, I still hated the exchange. I was starting to think of that dimple as mine. "Jax Williams. Nice to meet you."

"It's always nice to meet a man in uniform," she said, batting her long eyelashes at him.

I choked on my spit and doubled over coughing.

"Marion, are you okay?" Jax asked, placing a supportive hand on my back.

"Yeah," I said, sucking in air. "Just got something caught in my throat. I'll be fine."

"Your face is bright red. Maybe you should sit down for a minute." The concern in his tone made me want to do whatever he asked, but I just shook my head and straightened.

"It's okay. I'm fine, really," I said, though I was far from fine. My head was spinning with the events of the night. I just needed it to be over so that I could go home and regroup.

"It's lucky you showed up when you did," Lennon said, turning her attention back to Jax. "Without you, who knows how bad the fire would've been." She smiled softly at him. "Were you just driving by when you saw the commotion?"

"No," Jax said, sounding distracted as he continued to watch me. "I was on my way to the mixer."

"Oh," she said, her eyebrows rising up nearly to her hairline. "That's interesting." She tapped her finger against her lips. "This is just too good. I can't lock down my social media accounts now. My fans will go wild for this."

"For what?" I asked, shaking myself out of my uncalled-for-jealousy stupor.

"My options. Seriously. When I post about the three men I've chosen to trial date, they are going to go wild. I mean, come on. My options are an ex-boyfriend, a fireman, and a musician? This is the stuff of romance tropes. My fans are going to be so into this."

Bain, Bodhi, and... Jax? Bain and Bodhi were a perfect fit, but not Jax. If she'd been any other client, I would've tried to steer her toward someone other than Jax, but since he was the one who seemed to help change her mind, I couldn't. Not if it meant our partnership wasn't dead. "So you're not going to make everything private?" I asked, wondering if that was a good idea.

"Nope. I'll just post after each date, so no one has any idea where I'll be. In the meantime, I'll get a short-term rental or stay with a friend so that no one can follow me from home." She smiled happily and then beamed at Jax. "I can't wait for my date with you. I've never been out with a fireman before."

"Date?" Jax asked, but his gaze was locked on mine. He took a step closer to me and bent his head to whisper, "I never agreed to go on any dates. You didn't think I'd be one of your clients, did you?"

I quickly shook my head. "Of course not." Though I had invited him with the idea that I might set him up with someone. Possibly Bethany, but only if he was open to it. "Excuse us just a moment, Lennon," I said and dragged him a few feet away where we could talk without being overheard.

"What exactly is going on here, Marion?" Jax asked, his eyes narrowed in suspicion. "Are you seriously trying to fix me up with a social media celebrity?"

"No!" Dammit. That wasn't what I wanted at all. "I swear, I never had any intention of pairing you up with her." That was the truth. Jax wasn't the type of guy to put his life on display all over the internet. Besides, their auras weren't even a good match. "I invited you because I thought it might be a fun event."

"No you didn't. You might not have been planning to pair me up with Ms. Love over there, but I'm certain you had ideas of setting me up with someone. Someone who wasn't you. Am I right?"

There was no point in lying to him. Jax would see right through me. He always had. "Okay, yes. I thought you might meet someone who was better for you than me. Or decide to give Bethany a chance. Is it so wrong to want to see you happy?"

He closed his eyes and shook his head slowly. "You don't get it, do you? I *am* happy, Marion. I love my life. Despite the premise of your business, you must know that not everyone needs a partner to be happy, right?"

"Of course I know that. I don't have one and I'm happy!" I nearly shouted at him.

He gave me a blank stare. "If you say so."

"Asshole," I muttered.

Jax laughed. "There it is again. I've missed that feisty side of you."

I couldn't help my own chuckle. How was it that he always had the ability to make me laugh even if my day had gone to shit and I was pissed off at the world? My shoulders sagged as I sucked up my pride and gave him the apology he deserved. "I'm sorry for"—I waved a hand at the restaurant— "you know, trying to find you a date when you clearly don't need my help."

He glanced over his shoulder at Lennon. "You're right. I don't need your help, but it looks like you might need mine."

Dammit. "Yeah. I could use your help with this one. If Lennon makes her socials private, then my entire launch marketing plan goes to shit."

He nodded. "Okay then. I'll go on the date with her." His lips curved up into a half smile. "But only on one condition."

I raised one eyebrow, waiting.

"You have to have dinner with me."

"Jax," I said with a sigh. "Is this really how you want to get me to go out with you?"

His smile vanished as he shook his head. "No. Fuck." He ran a hand through his dark curls. "Fine. Don't worry about it. I'll go out with the internet queen, but only once. Then I'm out."

I stared at him, speechless for a moment. Finally, I asked, "Why?"

"You know why, Marion." Then he turned to walk away.

Without even thinking, I reached out and grabbed his wrist, stopping him.

He paused and glanced back at me.

"Okay. I'm free Tuesday night." The truth was, I was free every night the following week, but I needed a few days to get myself date-ready. I'd have to see if I could get an appointment at the spa and find something to wear that didn't make me look like I'd squeezed into a sausage casing. The past few years had been a little rough on my waistline.

His lips curved, giving me a glimpse of that dimple. "I'll pick you up at six."

I nodded, holding in a bubble of laughter. *Six o'clock.* Man, we'd gotten old. Back when we'd dated in high school, eight was considered early.

I watched him walk back over to Lennon. He had an easy smile for her, but it wasn't the same one he seemed to reserve for me. The one he gave her was friendly. The one he gave me was usually full of sex and mischief. That smile had gotten me into a lot of trouble back in the day. There was no doubt it still could.

"Oh, thank the gods," Iris said as she hurried over to me.

Jax was escorting Lennon to his truck. She was hanging all over his arm, but Jax wasn't looking at her. He was watching me. When our eyes met, a shiver of anticipation ran up my spine. Good gods, I wanted that man. I tore my gaze away and focused on Iris.

"Well. That's interesting, isn't it?" Her eyes twinkled with amusement.

"I don't know what you're talking about," I said with a shrug of indifference.

"Sure you don't." Smirking, she made a note in the little notebook she carried around with her.

"What did you just write down?" I demanded.

"Just that Jax Williams is taken," she said, her tone matter of fact.

"No, he isn't," I insisted. "We're just old friends."

"I believe you are old friends, but there is nothing *just* about it. That man wants you. And considering you look like you want to scratch Lennon's eyes out, I'm going out on a limb and saying you want him, too."

Why was everyone calling me out on my shit with Jax tonight? "Fine. I do. But we're not dating, and he's not taken. We aren't a good match."

"According to who?" she asked. "You?"

"Yes, me. Who else?"

"I don't know. I guess I figured being a matchmaker was kinda like being a therapist. No one should be diagnosing themselves."

"You're saying I'm not a good judge of who I should date?" I asked, a little offended.

"No, no," she said with a tiny chuckle. "I just meant that sometimes an outside opinion might be useful. Kinda like getting a second opinion on a bathing suit."

I groaned. "You did not just say that. Thank goodness it's January and I don't have to try to squeeze this body into a suit anytime soon."

Iris guffawed. "You look great. Now let's get out of here. We'll deal with the fallout of this tomorrow."

I followed her toward my car, but halfway there, I stopped in my tracks and hung my head.

"Marion?" Iris asked. "Are you okay?"

"Yeah. Or at least I will be. I think I just need to go home and get some rest. You're right. We can deal with everything else tomorrow."

"I'm sure everything will look better in the morning," Iris said as I waved goodnight.

I very much doubted it, but I admired her optimism.

CHAPTER 7

"*D*ad? Are you home?" I called as I strode into my cottage. His SUV was parked out front, but none of the lights were on in the garage apartment or in my house.

I walked straight to the kitchen and poured myself a glass of wine. But just as I pressed it to my lips, my head started to pound again, and I reluctantly poured it down the drain.

Could this night get any worse? After downing a couple of aspirin, I sipped my water and started to head toward my bedroom, but out of the corner of my eye, I saw movement on my back porch. My entire body tensed until my dad's tall frame came into view. He was in the shadows of the back porch, but I could still see him waving his arm in the air as he paced back and forth.

When I got closer, it was easier to see the phone pressed to his ear and the scowl on his face. I pulled the sliding glass door open and stood there as I listened to him rant to the person on the other end of the line.

Candy. His ex. It only took me a moment to know that was who he was talking to.

"Take that shit down off the internet immediately, or you'll be hearing from my lawyer," he demanded. There was a pause and then he continued. "I'll sue, because none of those things were mine!"

He threaded one hand into his hair and pulled at the ends, clearly frustrated beyond measure. "What would I sue for? What do you think? Defamation of character. I didn't even know what the hell a penis pump was, you cow. I had to look it up. Now I've got that in my search history. Thanks for that."

I heard cackling on the other end of the line before he pulled the phone away from his ear and jabbed at the screen, ending the call.

"That miserable bitch," he muttered to himself.

"At least I know where I get it from," I said, stepping out onto the porch to join him.

"Get what?"

"My potty mouth." I winked at him and slipped an arm around his waist to pull him in for a hug.

"That's probably not my best trait," he said, wrapping his arms around me for one of his famous bear hugs.

"It's better than your penchant for golden showers," I deadpanned.

"Marion," he growled. "Never say those words around me again."

I cackled and let him go. "Come on. Let's go inside and I'll show you how to block Candy from your page."

"I can do that?" he asked, eyeing me suspiciously.

"Yes. Do I need to sign you up for a social media class down at the senior center?" I teased.

"Hell. Maybe you do."

Twenty minutes later, with his laptop in front of me and

Candy's post successfully removed from Dad's page, we sipped a couple of decaf lattes.

"Do all your mixers turn out like that?" Dad asked, his lips twitching in amusement.

"Shut it, old man," I said, giving him the same shit he was giving me. "You know they don't."

"There were a handful of beautiful, interesting women to pick from. I'll give you that." He picked up his mug and brought it to his lips.

"Were any of them named Tazia?" I asked, trying to sound innocent.

Dad narrowed his eyes as he studied me. "Yes, as a matter of fact, I did find Tazia beautiful and interesting. But I'm not going to date her."

I let out a sigh that seemed like it had been lodged in my throat for hours. I'd known he'd say that. But just this once, I wished I'd been wrong. "Come on, Dad. Why won't you let me set you up with her? Is she too nice? Too classy? Too right for you?"

"Yes." He got up and headed toward the sink.

I was about to question him further when the doorbell rang. I glanced at the clock. It was well after midnight.

"Who comes over this late at night?" Dad asked. Then he turned to stare at me. "That's not a booty call, is it?"

"What? No." I rolled my eyes at him as I moved into the next room. "I don't do booty calls."

"Netflix and chill?" he called after me.

Shaking my head, I chuckled at his shenanigans. At least he wasn't boring. I pulled open the door and found Tazia standing there holding a ceramic bowl. "Tazia. What is it?"

"I couldn't sleep, so I brought you this cobbler. I made it

earlier today. I'm sorry to come by so late, but can I come in for a minute?"

"Of course." I stepped aside, waving her in.

"Dad!" I called. "There's cobbler to go with your latte."

He appeared in the doorway between the two rooms and leaned against the door jam.

"I know I should've waited until tomorrow, but I saw your lights on and..." Tazia gave me a helpless look.

"Don't worry about it. We're still up." I handed the cobbler to my dad. "Can you take this in the kitchen?"

"It's better if you warm it up," Tazia told him and then turned her attention to me again. "Are you feeling okay?"

"Physically? Yeah, sure. Why?" I sank down onto the couch and watched her as she paced the living room.

Tazia pressed her lips together in a thin line as she stared at the large picture window, but I knew she wasn't seeing anything but her own reflection. "I had a premonition of some kind." She shifted her gaze to me. "About you."

That cold dread was back, sending ice down my spine. A premonition? That didn't sound good. Especially if she was asking If I felt okay. "What was it?" I asked thickly.

"I saw you, standing here in this room, doubled over in pain, holding your head with both hands as if it were about to explode."

"A killer headache?" I automatically reached up to touch my temple with my fingers. My head was a little fuzzy and still a little tender, but the aspirin had done its job for the most part. I didn't feel like my brains were going to pound out of my head at least.

"Not just a headache. One that seemed to possess you. As if the only way to get rid of it was to exorcise it."

"Like a demon?" I asked, giving her a what-the-fuck look.

"Yes. Like that." She started to pace again, wringing her hands as she worked an imaginary hole in my throw rug.

"Uh, Tazia, are you saying you think I've been possessed by a demon?" My tone was teasing, but the way she flinched, she had me worried that was exactly what she was saying. "Wait. Do I need to go see an exorcist?"

She stopped the pacing, finally, and squinted at me. "I don't know. All I know is that something is off. Something big, but I can't put my finger on it."

"Tazia." My father's voice was firm and measured. "Thank you for the cobbler, but it's pretty late and I think we all need to get some rest."

She blinked at him. After a moment, she straightened her shoulders and nodded. "Right. It is late. I'm sorry to have bothered you. I just couldn't shake this feeling. I'm sure everything will look better in the morning."

I jumped up and cut her off before she strode out the front door. Grabbing her hands, I stared her in the eyes and said, "Thank you for coming. I really do feel okay, though. Maybe it's just the stress of the fire that's causing this… whatever it is."

"Maybe." She closed her eyes and took a deep breath as her hands tightened around my fingers. "But I don't really think so. I can feel the tumultuous energy radiating off you."

I glanced at my father, who was frowning at us with his brow furrowed. "Are you an empath?" he asked.

"No," Tazia said quickly, dropping my hands and taking a step back. "More like a seer, only it doesn't happen on demand." She eyed Dad and then walked over to him, taking his hands in hers, clasping them as she looked into his eyes.

"Well?" he asked.

She gazed up at him and then smiled softly. "Your energy is just fine." Her cheeks flushed as if she were shy or embarrassed. But I knew Tazia better than that. She wasn't a shy person, and normally she made zero apologies for who she was or what she felt.

I squinted at them. It was clear to my naked eyes that they were experiencing some sort of connection. It was obvious in the way they looked at each other. But their auras were way off. The previous evening, they'd merged a deep violet, making me sure they were the perfect match. But now, his had a burnt-orange tinge and hers was pale yellow with sepia-toned edges.

Since they were touching, shouldn't their auras be turning a deep shade of violet by now? Or maybe my father was right. It had been a long, stressful night. No one who had been at the fire was thinking about romance.

Sex maybe. Just for the release. But romance? No way. That was too much work right after almost burning down a local restaurant.

"I should go," Tazia said, breaking their eye contact.

"Right." Dad stuffed his hands in his pockets and took a step back. "Leave the demon to me. I'll take care of her."

I laughed.

Tazia glanced past my father and worry filled her chocolate eyes. "Just promise me you'll give me a call if you start to feel… different. Okay?"

"Different how?" I asked, confused.

"Just if you aren't feeling yourself. Or if you feel like you're no longer in control of your emotions. I know people who can help you."

I crossed my arms over my chest and shook my head. Tazia opened her mouth to protest, but I held one hand up, stopping her. "I have people, too."

I had an entire coven who'd come running if I needed someone.

They could deal with demons, right?

Right, I told myself as I waved goodnight to both Tazia and my father and prepared to fall into bed. Whatever was trying to consume my soul would have to wait until I got eight solid hours of sleep.

Then it'd have a fight on its hands.

And I'd be ready.

CHAPTER 8

*M*y head throbbed, and my queasy stomach protested when I brought the mug of coffee to my lips. I let out a groan and placed the mug on my desk without taking a sip.

"What have I done to deserve this?" I asked the empty office. I'd woken up just past dawn, feeling like I'd been on a complete bender the night before. After trying unsuccessfully to sleep off the headache, I'd finally gotten out of bed and dragged myself to work, hoping that if I pretended I felt normal, that I could fake it until I made it.

No such luck.

My phone buzzed with a text and I squinted at it.

Tandy: *Holy shit, Mar. I heard about the fire. What happened? And why didn't you call me last night?*

Grimacing, I tapped out a response. *Sorry. Long night. I'm fine. No one was hurt. Call you later to catch up?*

Tandy: *You better, or I'll be blowing up your phone.*

She would, too. Tandy was the type of friend who was

always present for those she cared about. And somehow, she always managed to be there when she was needed the most. We almost never texted during business hours. Her days were packed with meetings for her multiple projects, but it didn't surprise me that she took a moment to check on me. Not after what had happened last night.

The front door swung open and Iris walked in, carrying a bag from the Bird's Eye Bakery. "I've come with reinforcements," she said, keeping her voice low. She placed the bag on my desk and said, "There's sourdough toast for now and a pumpkin pastry for later if you're feeling up to it." A paper cup joined the bag. "And this is herbal tea from Gigi. She said it will help settle your stomach and clear up your headache."

"Bless you both." I gave her a grateful smile and picked up the tea. There was hardly any scent, making me appreciate Gigi even more. The woman certainly knew what she was doing in the herb department. Between her and Carly, I should've already had a remedy for my pseudo hangover, but I was so rarely sick, stocking up on restorative remedies hadn't even occurred to me.

"Are you sure something didn't get slipped into your drink?" Iris asked, sitting across from me with concern in her light blue eyes. "This doesn't happen after just one glass of champagne."

"I don't think so, but considering I feel like death, it certainly would explain things." Or maybe Tazia had been onto something when she'd said I was possessed by a demon. That would be enough to take anyone down, wouldn't it? I took a sip of the tea. Its mild flavor didn't turn my stomach, and encouraged by the progress, I took another longer sip. The effect was almost immediate. The pounding in my skull slowed to a dull ache, and although I was still exhausted, I could at least finally look at my computer screen without the room spinning.

"It's working," Iris said, sounding pleased.

"It is. Thank you."

"Thank the gods. Maybe it's just a twenty-four-hour bug that's no match for Gigi's tea."

I nodded and pulled the pastry bag toward me. Bread was one of the things I'd been trying to cut out to help me lose weight, but desperate times called for desperate measures. I hadn't been able to get any food down yet, and sourdough toast sounded like just the thing to settle my stomach. I'd definitely eat the pumpkin pastry later. There was no point in wasting food was there?

"Have you read Lennon's social media posts yet?" Iris asked.

"No. My eyes weren't focusing." I tapped my laptop awake and clicked the shortcut I'd already saved that led to Lennon's page.

I let out a groan when I spotted the picture of the firetruck and an ambulance outside of Witches' Garden. The headline read, *When I asked the universe for a smokin' hot date, I didn't mean it literally!*

"You have to admit her headline skills are on point," I said without any enthusiasm. I absolutely did not want my business to be associated with almost burning down a restaurant. But it wasn't as if I could ask her not to provide that detail. Surely the incident had made the local news, and people would find it online soon enough.

"It's not as bad as you think," Iris said, getting up and moving over to the office espresso machine.

"That's probably not that high of a bar to reach," I said, considering I was expecting the worst.

Dear People of the Page,

Last night was the Miss Matched mixer for the meet and greet. As you can see, things took an unexpected turn. Not only was there a fire, but the fire was also started by some man who was rambling about a penis pump!

Yes, you read that right. A man at the mixer was talking about his penis pump. Or rather, he was denying he had one after someone on social media accused him of leaving his behind. I don't know that story, but you haven't lived until a man starts a fire just to get people to stop accusing him of needing help to get his equipment going.

Anyway, as near as I can tell, the fire was an accident and no one was hurt. Thank the gods. Up until the flames ran us out of the restaurant, I was pleasantly surprised to find I was enjoying myself. Swipe for pictures of me in my latest look as I charmed all the men at my table. *wink*

But when I got outside, I found an ugliness no one deserves. Keep swiping for the graffiti left on my car. I'll be honest and tell you that when I saw this ugliness, I was ready to shut down my social media pages. Every public figure has to deal with asshats on the internet, but this is different. I can't just block someone who followed me to a public event and then spray-painted this nastiness. It's violating and horrifying to know that someone was motivated enough to do this.

I was fully prepared to lock down my accounts until the perpetrator has been caught, but I've since decided I can't let anyone take away my joy and my livelihood. As such, I'll be taking pains to be more careful about posting where I am or where I'll be, and you'll be getting updates after the fact. I probably should've been doing that to begin with, so this is just a new policy of mine.

So please stay to hear all about my adventures both big and small.

See my next post for an update on where I go from here with Miss Matched Midlife Dating Agency!

I glanced at Iris. "I could've done without the mention of the penis pump, but all things considered, this is about the best I could've hoped for."

She nodded and grinned. "Read the next post."

I scrolled to the newest post and my eyes nearly bugged out when I saw the comments were already in the tens of thousands. "This can't be real."

"This is pure gold. You will flip when you see how many inquiries have come through on the website already this morning."

"Seriously?" I raised my eyebrows, my fingers itching to flip over to our website's contact email, but I refrained. I needed to know what Lennon had posted before I did anything else.

"Seriously. It's even better than I'd hoped for." Iris sat back and kicked her feet up on the desk with her hands clasped behind her head.

With my mysterious hangover under control and Iris practically giddy with the promise of new clients, today was definitely looking up.

I turned my attention to Lennon's latest post.

It's time to vote! Help a girl out, will you? I've been matched with these three hot guys. Marion Matched really hit it out of the park, don't you think? Not only are they droolworthy, but each one is accomplished in their chosen careers. We're talking the entire package.

No, not that package, you pervs. Keep your minds out of the gutter.

I'm talking about men who have their shit together and also happen to look like GQ cover models. But that brings its own challenges. Like how I'm ever going to be able to choose between these three hotties. Let me know in the comments who you prefer: the firefighter, the musician, or.... drumroll... an ex who got away? That's right, folks. Marion Matched found someone I've loved and lost before. Is there hope for a second-chance romance in my future? Or maybe I'm meant to spend time with the man who'll light my fire. But then the thought of being played like an instrument by the musician might prove to be too tempting.

Don't be shy. Tell me who you'd pick.

There were photos of each of the men, taken in profile in such a way that their facial features were mostly obscured. Honestly, the photos were genius. All three looked sexy as hell, but identifying them would prove to be pretty difficult for the masses.

I glanced at the comments and felt my lips curving into a pleased smile. The votes for the different men were all over the board. And I was pleased to see that while the fireman was popular, most were pulling for the musician. Of course they were. With that line *played like an instrument,* she'd primed them for that one.

"This post is brilliant," I told Iris.

"It really is. Lennon Love is worth every penny you're paying her. Go take a look at the Miss Matched Midlife Dating Agency page. Check out the swell of new users following us."

My old social media page for my business that I'd had in LA had a healthy following, but the new one for The Miss Matched Midlife Dating Agency only had a few dozen prior to the mixer. But now? There were over two thousand followers, and the count was only continuing to grow. Plus, there were a lot of comments on the announcement for the mixer, most of them asking to be fixed up with the fireman, the musician or to help them find their one that got away. Everyone was a sucker for their first love.

"What the...?" I turned to Iris. "This is insane."

"It really is." She took a long sip of her coffee and then added, "Should we get to work?"

There was no time like the present.

71

CHAPTER 9

$\mathcal{F}$our hours later, we'd gone through all the inquiries on the website, signed over a dozen new clients, and I went to work on scheduling Lennon with Jax, Bodhi, and Bain on their solo dates. I'd scheduled Jax first, since I knew they weren't a good match and the first meetings that clients went on usually didn't turn out as well as one might hope. They were usually too nervous to relax. Plus, I just wanted to get it out of the way so that I didn't have to think about it anymore. Once I was done scheduling Lennon's dates, I turned to Iris.

"How about lunch? I think I'm going to need something other than a pumpkin pastry."

"Sure. Kade just messaged and said he's over at Pointe of View Café. We could meet him there."

I frowned. "I don't want to interrupt your lunch date. You go on ahead. I'll order a salad or something."

"No way," she said, already getting to her feet. "It's not a date. He's there with Lucas. Come on. Save me from being overwhelmed by manly men who've been working with their bare hands, making furniture all morning."

I laughed. "Okay. When you put it like that, how can I say no?"

"You can't." She grabbed her jacket and her keys. "Come on. I'm suddenly starving."

Ten minutes later when we walked into the café, Iris made a beeline for the back of the restaurant. It took me a moment to register who all was at our table. Kade, Iris's boyfriend, Lucas, Hope's fiancé, and Owen, Grace's boyfriend.

"What do we have here?" I asked as I slid onto one of the chairs. "Looks like a boys' lunch. We aren't interrupting, are we?"

"Hell no," Kade said, slipping his arm around Iris. "You two just made this lunch bearable."

Iris grinned down at him and placed her hand on the back of his neck. "That was sweet."

The other two men made immature kissing noises as they gave the couple hell, but I wasn't paying any attention. Instead, I was staring at Kade and Iris. I'd seen them together more times than I could count. Every time, their auras had melded to be a lovely shade of violet that was tinted magenta at the edges.

Today, there wasn't a hint of either color. Iris's aura was a deep red, and Kade's was a light blue. Most importantly, they were both brown at the edges, just like Tazia's and my father's had been the night before.

I blinked and studied them closer, wondering what would happen if I waited a few more minutes. Would the brown edges start to fade or intensify? And what exactly did it mean? This hadn't ever happened to me before.

My heart started to race while my palms turned sweaty.

"Marion?" Iris said, worry in her tone. "What's wrong?"

"I'm not exactly sure," I hedged.

Iris glanced behind her and then around the restaurant. "What am I missing here?"

I let out a sigh and ran a hand through my auburn-dyed curls. It was a sign of how disoriented I was. A woman with natural curls almost never tried to finger-comb her locks. Not unless she wanted to deal with a frizzy mess. "It's your auras. They're... off."

"What do you mean, off?" Lucas asked at the same time Owen said, "You can see auras?"

Obviously Grace hadn't filled him in on my special talent. "Yes," I said. "Yours is a pale shade of orange right now." And again, the edges were tinged brown.

"What does that mean?" he asked, sounding curious.

I shrugged. "It could be any number of things, but I'm not the one to ask about that anyway. I only read compatibility when it comes to auras, and if I had just met Iris and Kade today, I'd conclude that they were a terrible match."

There was silence at the table as everyone looked from me to Iris and Kade and back again.

"Oops," I said. "I didn't mean to blurt it out like that. Of course you're perfect for each other. I've seen it many times with my own eyes. This"—I waved a hand in their direction —"is an anomaly. I saw the same thing happen with my dad and Tazia last night. I thought it was just because I was tired and so were they. But now..." I trailed off, wondering what was happening. Why were all the love matches around me starting to fall apart?

"You're saying our auras aren't melding the way they do when people are a good match?" Iris asked me.

I nodded. "And the edges are turning brown, like there's not enough energy to keep your aura at full-strength."

"I'm not even sure what that means," Iris said quietly.

"It's okay. All you need to know is that my aura-reading gift isn't working correctly. Either that, or everyone who is in love has been cursed."

"Cursed?" Iris said. "That can't be, can it?" She squeezed Kade's shoulder, and he placed one of his hands over hers.

"If we're cursed, then I'm glad we're cursed together," Kade said, winking at her.

Owen and Lucas both groaned.

"Dude," Lucas said. "That's enough cheese to clog an artery."

Kade shrugged one shoulder. "It was a good line, though, right?"

Iris chuckled. "Definitely."

"Hey! We made it," Grace called as she hurried to the table with Hope right behind her.

"Sorry we're late." Hope leaned down and kissed Lucas on the cheek. "Grace over here just had to get her eyebrows waxed. She said something about caterpillars crawling on her face. Then there was the lip wax, eyelash tinting, and a threat of a pedicure, but that's when I put my foot down and demanded she feed me lunch before she committed to anymore spa treatments."

Chatter rose up around me as the six friends talked about the excitement from the night before. I quickly tuned them out and focused first on Grace and Owen and then on Hope and Lucas.

My head started to ache again as my stomach churned.

There was no denying the obvious. The table was filled with three happy couples. Couples whose auras I'd seen numerous times. They were all deeply compatible with each other.

76

And yet today, their auras made them all look like their relationships were in big trouble.

I knew in my gut that they weren't the problem. The issue was me.

My gift was gone.

CHAPTER 10

"What do you mean your gift is gone?" Iris demanded.

I'd been quiet for most of the rest of the lunch. It wasn't until after the men left that the three coven members had turned their undivided attention to me. Now we were at the coven circle overlooking Premonition Pointe with the waves churning at the bottom of the cliff. Grace had put in a call to the rest of the coven members, and we were just waiting for them to arrive.

"It's just vanished. I noticed it last night but brushed it off. Then today, when I saw you all with your significant others, it was clear. I can no longer count on my aura-reading ability to recognize relationship connections. That part is just... gone." I swallowed hard as I thought of Tazia and her warning.

Demon.

Was I possessed for real? I hadn't given her concerns any serious thought at first. As far as I was concerned, demon possession was a thing that only happened in the movies, not in Premonition Pointe to a middle-aged matchmaker. Why would a demon take over my body instead of someone hotter, more flexible, and with a ton more energy?

"Gifts don't just vanish into thin air," Grace said thoughtfully. "Maybe something is jamming your readings?"

"Like power lines or maybe a demon possession?" I asked flippantly. I hadn't meant to mention the demon thing. Surely I wasn't possessed. I hadn't tried to claw anyone's eyes out or barfed up something that looked like pea soup.

"Demon?" Grace asked, sounding cautious.

The other two rolled their eyes. Hope was the first to speak. "I think jumping straight to demon possession is a little dramatic, don't you?"

"Sure," I said, still unable to bring myself to tell them about Tazia's warning. "I just don't want to leave any stone unturned."

Gigi Martin arrived, suddenly popping out from behind a redwood tree. "What's this I hear about demons?" She glanced around the circle, nodding to each of her friends before holding my gaze for a long moment. "Your energy is different, Marion. Heavier and with tinges of something sticky. Something's wrong, isn't it?"

I nodded at the other woman, more certain than ever that Tazia might have actually been correct.

Gigi walked over to me, her white linen dress blowing in the breeze behind her. She always had an ethereal vibe about her. I thought maybe it was her connection to the earth and the fact that she lived in a house with the ghosts of her ancestors. She just seemed to be more in tune with the spiritual plane. She slipped her hand into mine, and immediately her eyes widened, filling with shock and worry.

"Oh hell. I really am possessed, aren't I?" I blurted. "Tazia said I might be, but I didn't take her seriously. Even in

Hollywood, I've never known anyone to be possessed. And if a demon was looking for a soul to corrupt, that's the place to do it."

A soft chuckle came from behind me, and I turned to see Carly Preston and Joy Lansing standing there. Carly was a bona fide movie star and an old friend who'd been in the business for decades. Joy had just started her acting career and had gotten her big break when she'd starred in a movie with Carly recently. Carly stood on my other side from where Gigi was and said, "I can think of a few people who were most likely possessed. It would explain a lot."

I gave her a sad smile. "I guess that's true. But mostly I just think those people were power-drunk assholes."

"You have a point." She glanced at Gigi. "Do you feel that?"

Gigi nodded. "Her energy is… heavy. Like it's being bogged down."

"Yes, that's a good description," Carly agreed.

"I didn't feel great when I woke up. It's probably just me needing more sleep," I said, though I wasn't sure why I was trying to explain away what they felt. Maybe I just really wanted to believe that there wasn't a baddie from the dark side trying to consume my soul.

"It's not that," Gigi said. "It feels like magic."

Iris let out a gasp. "You think she's been tagged by a curse?"

"It's certainly possible," Gigi said.

Carly nodded her agreement.

"Should we call the Magical Task Force?" Iris asked, already pulling out her phone.

"What's that?" I asked, frowning at her.

"It's the agency that investigates all unusual paranormal activity," Hope said. She gave me an encouraging smile. "If you are harboring a demon, they'd be the people to call."

"Do it," I ordered Iris. "Whatever is happening to me, I want the professionals on it."

"Okay." Iris tapped her screen and waited for someone to pick up. Time seemed to stand still as she held the phone to her ear and grimaced. After a few moments, she smiled and said her hellos to the rep on the other end of the connection. She quickly explained the situation and then frowned. "What do you mean, low priority? What if my friend has been cursed?"

I bit down on the side of my cheek as I listened to the rapidly deteriorating phone call.

"No. She doesn't appear to be in any immediate danger. No, she's not a danger to anyone else. But—" She let out a frustrated sigh. "As I was trying to say—"

Gigi squeezed my hand. I glanced up at her, grateful for the support.

"So we're just supposed to sit around and wait for someone to become available?" Iris asked, sounding exasperated. "I guess we don't have a choice, do we?" She ended the call and turned to me, her expression heated. "They're too short staffed. Apparently, unless you're bleeding from your eyeballs, no one is available to investigate a possible curse."

"Of course not," I muttered. Customer service across the board seemed to be nonexistent these days. It'd taken nearly a month just to get my internet turned on at the office. Not to mention there'd been a recording error on my latest house payment, and I was still fighting the bank to get it cleared up. Why had I thought the Magical Task Force would be any different?

"We don't need them," Gigi said.

Everyone turned to look at her. She was staring out toward the ocean, her gaze unfocused.

"Uh, Gigi?" Joy asked. "What are you saying?"

Gigi blinked her warm amber eyes and focused on the tall, model-thin blonde. "We're a coven, right? We can do a spell to reveal the curse or, at worst, the demon."

"Whoa!" Hope held her hands up in front of her. "I think summoning a demon is a little out of our wheelhouse, don't you?"

The other coven members voiced their agreement, some of them looking agitated.

"We're not going to be summoning a demon," Gigi said, shaking her head. "We're just going to ask the goddess to help us see what's blocking Marion's energy."

"Oh. Well, that's okay," Hope said with a one-shoulder shrug. "That makes more sense."

Grace sat back down next to Hope and said, "Leave it to you to go full drama queen."

Hope just laughed. From what I knew about her, she actually was one of the most laid-back members of the coven. She never gave me drama vibes.

Gigi clapped her hands together. "Let's go, coven. We have work to do."

I sat on a log and watched as they all jumped into action. Candles appeared, a salt circle was formed, and one of them produced a pestle and mortar along with a variety of herbs.

"Marion, sit here." Gigi waved to a log in the middle of the circle.

Grace handed me a thick white pillar candle. "Hold this."

With both hands wrapped around the candle, I sat on the log, watching my friends move as if they were performing a choreographed dance. They each held candles and walked around the circle, lifting and lowering their unlit candles in a synchronized fashion.

83

Then they all paused and turned inward toward the circle, and Gigi said, "Goddess of the earth, wind, sea, and sun, ignite our offerings and illuminate our gathering."

Every candle, including mine, flickered to life with a soft flame.

The coven held their candles out, and in unison they dropped their hands, leaving the candles suspended in front of each of them.

"Release your candle, Marion," Gigi said softly.

I glanced down at the candle in my hands and tried to ignore the nervousness coursing through my body. I didn't have the sort of magic the coven members did. If I let go, would it float in the air or tumble down into my lap with the flame still flickering in the soft breeze?

"Trust us," Gigi said, sounding kind and patient.

I nodded once, and keeping a close eye on the candle, I slowly released it. As soon as it was free of my grasp, it rose in the air, hovering at the same level as the other six.

Gigi raised her arms in the air. The coven mimicked her movements, and they all started chanting.

"Goddess of the earth, wind, sea, and sun, hear our call."

They repeated the phrase three times before Gigi took over and said, "Show us the secrets Marion carries in the shadows."

I swallowed. My secrets? Did that mean they were going to learn about that time Jax and I had been arrested for public indecency? Or the time I'd stolen a pint of ice cream from the corner store on the night Jax and I had broken up for good? But could they blame me? I was broke and needed comfort. Plus, the owner was a jerk who'd once taken a dog to the pound because he was too lazy to call the number on his tag.

Even though the day had been clear, suddenly the clouds rolled in and a rumble of thunder sounded overhead. The wind picked up and the six coven members straightened, their arms held high in the air, looking powerful and larger than life.

The clouds parted and light streamed down through the opening. My skin started to tingle, and then magic was coating my skin. All the coven members' auras came into crisp focus, each one bright white except for the singed brown edges. The longer I stared at them, the more pronounced the brown edges became.

Gigi dropped her arms, and the other women mimicked her movement. All the pillar candles floated to the ground, and when they touched the earth, the flames went out. The clouds cleared, leaving us all bathed in the California sun as a slight breeze sent goosepimples over my flesh.

I blinked at Gigi. "What just happened?"

"The goddess revealed what's ailing you," she said, slowly lowering herself to one of the logs. The other coven members followed, but none of them said a word.

I glanced around at their stony faces and felt that pit in my stomach return. "It's a demon, isn't it?"

Gigi's lips twitched in amusement, but she quickly schooled her features. "No. There's no demon."

The tension instantly drained from my body. Whatever it was, at least I wouldn't be trying to eat my own flesh from the inside out. "Okay. That's a relief. Then what's with the long faces?"

They exchanged looks with each other but didn't say anything. Instead, they all looked to Gigi to give me the bad news.

"Gigi," I said with a sigh. "Just tell me. Did you guys have a premonition of something terrible happening to me or what?" That would be just my luck. Finally land in a town I absolutely adored and get my business up and running, only to drop dead of a heart attack.

Chuckling, Gigi shook her head. "Do you always blurt out what's on your mind?"

"When I'm nervous, yes," I admitted.

She nodded. "I get that. Well, I can't say the nerves aren't warranted. Did you see that magic coating your skin?"

"Yes. I thought that was from you six."

"That would make things a lot easier if it had been," she said with a sigh. "This is a curse."

I sucked in a sharp breath. I'd always known that was a possibility. "All right. How do we get rid of it? That's something you guys can do, right?"

Gigi stared right at me, sucked in a breath, and said, "No. I'm sorry, Marion, but it's permanent."

CHAPTER 11

"What?" I jumped up off the log and turned, taking in the expression of each of the coven members. "This can't be true. Surely there's an anti-curse or some sort of potion that can neutralize this—whatever it is."

"I wish there was," Carly said, stepping up beside Gigi. "But the curse that's clinging to you is not superficial. None of us are powerful enough to break it."

"But what if you joined forces? You just made the clouds part and the thunder roll," I said, waving to the sky. "You can't break one curse? I don't even know where I got it. Shouldn't it have hurt or something?"

I turned to Iris. "Don't you have your father's amulet? It has to be powerful enough to reverse this thing." Iris was the only one of us who had a magical device that carried that type of power. She rarely used it, and as far as I knew, she kept it locked away safely where others couldn't get to it easily.

Iris bit down on her bottom lip and slowly shook her head. "It doesn't really have that kind of accuracy. I'm afraid I'd end up hurting you if I tried to do something like that. It's more of a blunt-force type of thing instead of a tool to do precision work like breaking curses."

"That sucks," I said, throwing my hands up and trying to ignore the panic that was churning in my gut.

"I'll do some research, though," Iris offered. "Find out if there's any history of amulets breaking curses without hurting anyone."

I slowly let out a breath. "Okay. That seems reasonable. Thank you."

"I'll start listening in around town," Hope said. "I'm sure my mom will be on board to help, too. Helping others is just about the only time she's grateful for her gift." Both Hope and her mother had the ability to listen in on other people's thoughts, but Angela's power was much stronger. She normally hated using her gift, but finding someone who was going around cursing people was probably right in her wheelhouse.

I reached out and squeezed Hope's hand. "Thank you."

Joy moved closer to me. "This had to have happened last night, right? Or this morning?"

"Definitely last night. I noticed it when Tazia came by around midnight. I was still seeing aura compatibility during the mixer," I said, pressing my fingers to my temples. "I don't know. I'm must've been cursed sometime between when the fire broke out and when I got home."

Grace let out a gasp. "There was some sort of flash of light right when your dad started to climb on the table. I thought it was strange but forgot all about it in all the excitement. It definitely looked like some sort of spell."

We were all silent as we took that in.

"You think someone did it at the mixer?" Iris asked Grace.

Grace shrugged. "That's my guess. Anyone have any better ideas?"

Everyone shook their heads. Then they looked at me.

I held my hands out, palms up. "I did hear *something*. Like a bang right when that woman in the floral dress took me down. It's as good a theory as any, I suppose." We were all silent and I realized we were all taking in what I'd said. "The woman in the floral dress. That's where we need to start, right?" I asked.

They all murmured their agreement.

Iris frowned. "I didn't recognize her. Did you?"

I shook my head. "No. But that's not that unusual. I often invite people who are on the vetted list to those things even if I don't think they're the perfect fit, because you never really know."

"I think that's where we start," Carly said, moving to sit next to me and take my hand in hers. "Find out who she is, and then start asking questions."

"That sounds like a good plan, but we can't be certain it was her. I mean, my dad was the one who knocked her into me, remember?"

Joy nodded. "Then we need to start investigating all of the guests."

"Any ideas on how to do that?" I asked, feeling more than a little skeptical. I didn't love the idea of putting every Miss Matched client on the suspect list. But if it were true that someone cursed me at the mixer, what choice did we have?

"I can start by looking at photos of everyone who was there," Joy said.

I frowned at her. "What would you be looking for?"

"Visions," Carly said quietly. "Joy saw my niece get abducted a while back, and she is the reason Harlow is back safely with me."

Right. I'd heard that, though I didn't think it was public

89

knowledge. The coven kept things close to the vest. "That's remarkable."

"Just know that I can't control the visions or force them to come," Joy said. "I'll try, but no promises. Though they have been happening more often, lately. Unfortunately, those glimpses are usually things I don't really want to see. You haven't lived until you get a flash of your costar manscaping." She shivered and glanced down at her crotch. "It gives a new meaning to the term *dick pics.*"

An unexpected chuckle escaped my lips. "That sounds… interesting."

"You can say that again," Hope muttered from beside Joy.

I held Joy's gaze. "I appreciate the offer, and I'll take any help I can get."

Carly and Gigi offered to put their heads together and try to create some sort of revealing spell while Grace said she'd keep an ear out around town. As a realtor, she heard all kinds of things, and not always from the living. Currently, she was the go-to realtor when a place was haunted.

Iris pulled out her phone and started tapping in notes. "I'll start by making a database of everyone who was there last night." She turned to me. "Then we can take a look into their backgrounds and see if there are any red flags. Anything that would help us pinpoint who did this and why."

I nodded, grateful for them all. Tears stung my eyes. "Thank you all so much for figuring out I've been cursed and doing everything you can to help me fix it. I just… I don't know what will happen if my gift doesn't come back."

Iris reached out and squeezed my hand. "You're going to be okay. I've seen you work. It's not all about your magic and their auras. You also have a knack for reading people. You'll see. I promise."

No matter what Iris said, I knew how much I relied on my aura-reading ability. Without it, I'd just be another matchmaker, setting people up on dates and hoping for the best. That wasn't the type of service I promised. If the curse wasn't lifted, my entire life would be turned upside down and I could kiss the Miss Matched Midlife Dating Agency goodbye. And then what? How would I support myself? Open a café or a gift shop? There certainly wasn't anything wrong with either of those choices, they just weren't me.

I was a matchmaker. A magical one. Without my gift, I had no idea who I was.

"Marion?" Iris asked.

I met her gaze and waited.

"You're going to be okay. Understand?"

"Yeah, okay," I said, because what else was I going to do? Have a meltdown right there at the coven circle in front of the women I admired most? No way. I'd wait until I got home to lose my shit.

CHAPTER 12

$\mathcal{I}$ walked into the cottage and headed straight to the kitchen. There was no hesitation. No guilt. No justifying anything. I'd had a shit day, and there wasn't anything that could fix it. But that didn't mean I couldn't make myself feel better.

The Pop-Tarts were right where I'd left them on the top shelf of the cabinet on the right. I ripped open the silver wrapping, tossed them into the toaster, and stood there waiting for the sweet aroma of brown sugar and cinnamon to fill my kitchen.

"You know what goes perfect with Pop-Tarts?"

I turned to find Celia the ghost leaning against the counter, her arms crossed over her chest.

"A hot man to feed them to me?"

Her lips curved into a half smile. "Yeah, that's better than what I was going to say, but since I don't see one here, you'll just have to make us lattes."

"Us?" I asked with one eyebrow raised.

"Yes, us. I might not be able to eat anything, but I can still smell it. And I highly doubt you're going to let me sniff yours."

Chuckling, I walked over to the Nespresso and got my latte started.

When the Pop-Tarts popped out of the toaster, my stomach rumbled with anticipation. Without waiting for them to cool, I tore a piece off the end and shoved it into my mouth. The brown sugar melted on my tongue, and I let out a groan of satisfaction.

"I hate you right now," Celia said, eyeing my pastry as if she wanted to make love to it.

"Damn, this is delicious." I licked my fingers and then took another bite before finishing up my latte.

"Hey!" Celia protested. "What about me?"

I poured some of mine into a mug for her and set it on the counter. "Sniff away."

Standing next to each other in the kitchen, Celia sniffed the latte like a drug dog at LAX while I slowed down and took my time, savoring my Pop-Tarts.

"Tell me about the ghost at the mixer," I said. "New friend?"

"New client," she said. "He's looking for a date. I told him I'm a matchmaker, and he promised to show me how to swap my clothes and taste food again if I find him a date."

"And you believed him?" I asked, feeling more than a little skeptical.

"I watched his clothes morph from jeans and a T-shirt to that suit he was wearing, so yeah, I think he's telling the truth." She tilted her head back and stared at the ceiling. "Besides, if he's a liar, what difference does it make? It's not like I need payment in the form of cash. I just want to know how to live a better ghostly existence."

There was a wistfulness to her tone that made me want to

squeeze her hand or give her a hug. Instead, I settled for letting her sniff my Pop-Tart.

She sighed her satisfaction and said, "You might be the best boss ever."

When Jax walked in a minute later, we were both still standing next to each other, moaning our satisfaction as we gave our afternoon treats our complete attention.

"Should I come back?" he asked, already moving backward through the doorway.

"What? No," I said around my mouthful of yummy goodness. "There's no reason to leave."

"Are you sure? It sounded like you were having a moment with…" He squinted and then laughed. "Are you eating Pop-Tarts?"

"Yes." Gobbling down the last bite, I grabbed my latte, and on my way to the table, I gestured to the fridge. "Help yourself if you want something to drink."

Jax nodded, did as I instructed, and then sat next to me after he'd popped the cap on a bottle of beer.

I eyed the local lager and wondered when my father had purchased it. I wasn't much of a beer drinker, so it wasn't mine. "Pretty sure that's my dad's. He might expect repayment."

"No doubt," Jax said with a laugh. "Don't worry. I'm good for it."

We sat in silence as we each sipped our drinks.

Celia, who'd been staring at us, heaved a heavy sigh. "Dammit, the tension in here is enough to drive a girl to drink. Too bad I can't start knocking back shots."

"What tension?" I asked at the same time Jax set his beer bottle on the table and reached for my hand. I stared at his fingers covering mine and then raised my gaze to his.

"That tension." Celia shook her head. "Also, could you tone down whatever this is?" She waved her hand at us. "If your auras were any more purple, I'd have to scratch my eyes out."

"What?" I whipped my head around and stared wide-eyed at her.

"Purple always reminds me of my mother and that horrible trailer I grew up in. Everything was purple. And I do mean everything. The couch, the ratty bean bag chair, the dishes, the carpet, the shower curtain she used as a curtain over the sliding glass door. It was worse than when she went through her incense stage." The ghost visibly shuddered.

"You're just fucking with me," I said with a finality that didn't require an answer.

Still she shrugged one shoulder. "If you say so. But if I were still alive, I'd show you the pictures. It's like someone threw up grape juice all over that trailer."

"That's not—"

"Knock, knock!" Tazia's familiar voice carried in through the screen door.

"Come on in, Tazia," I called back and listened as the door creaked open and her footsteps fell on the hardwood floor.

"Oh, I didn't realize you had visitors," she said when she spotted Jax and Celia. She was holding a bouquet of deep red tulips.

"I'm not a visitor, really," Celia said. "More like a coworker. Also Marion owes me a date."

Tazia's gaze shifted between me and the ghost. "Is that a new service, then? Helping people who have already crossed over?"

"No." I rose and walked over to Tazia.

Celia let out a huff of irritation. "You said you'd help me."

I glanced back at her. "I said I'd help if I could. Which is questionable. Matching people in the afterlife certainly isn't in my business plan." Although, maybe I should remain open to the idea. If I couldn't see auras anymore, I was going to have to get creative.

Tazia handed me the flowers and said, "They're from my greenhouse."

"For me?" I asked, delighted.

"Of course for you? Who else, Celia?" she asked with a laugh.

"Hey! I like flowers. Though I'm more of a long-stem roses kind of a girl," Celia said with a pout. "It's been ages since I've been able to bat these eyelashes at a man until he can't resist sending me two dozen with the hopes for a coffee date."

I rolled my eyes at my ghost and took the flowers from Tazia. Reaching for her to give her a hug, I whispered, "Thank you. They're gorgeous. It was very kind of you to bring them over. And just so you know, I'm not possessed. The coven confirmed it."

She pulled back and stared me in the eye. I was certain she didn't believe me, but then she nodded and whispered back, "Okay. Thanks for telling me. But there is something, right? Like a spell or curse?"

I nodded solemnly. "We're working on it."

Tazia pulled me into another tight hug. "I'm here if you need me."

"I know." I squeezed my eyes shut and held on until I heard footsteps on my hardwood floors.

"I didn't realize there was a party going on," My dad said, walking up behind Tazia.

Tazia shifted and gave him a sweet smile. One that was almost shy. "Hi, Memphis. How are you today?"

"Better than I was last night." He walked over to the counter and grabbed a cookie out of the cookie jar. He offered one to everyone, but Tazia was the only one who took him up on it.

"Ugh. Those two need to leave. I can't take this much purple," Celia demanded as she gestured to Tazia and my dad. "It's enough to make a girl want to puke."

"Good thing you're past that bodily function," I said dryly. But then I took a long look and my dad and Tazia. Their auras were faded, hers pale yellow and his pale orange. No purple in sight. "Celia, are you just fucking with me?"

"I'd say that's a strong possibility," Jax said with a chuckle. "Isn't that her only reason for visiting you these days?"

"Please, I'm a working girl now," Celia said with an air of superiority. "You'll see. I'm going to help her make Miss Matched a roaring success."

"My apologies," Jax said solemnly. "I didn't mean to offend."

She waved a hand in his direction, dismissing his apology. "Please. Two days ago, you'd have been right." She winked one of her big eyes at him. "Marion's just a fun target. Who can resist?"

"Celia, we need to talk," I said, already moving into the living room.

"About what?" she called from her spot in the kitchen.

"Just get out here," I ordered and flopped down onto the couch, closing my eyes. How had my home turned into Grand Central Station when I hadn't invited even one of them to visit?

"Rough day?" a welcome and familiar voice asked.

My eyes flew open and I spotted Ty standing there with his dark hair windblown and a suitcase at his feet. "Ty!" I jumped up and wrapped him in my arms, giving him the tightest bear hug, I could manage. "Why didn't you tell me you were on your way?"

"I wanted it to be a surprise," he said over my shoulder. "Looks like my plan worked."

I let out a happy chuckle, pulled away, and just stared into his handsome face. He'd been so broken when Trish died in that car accident four years ago. So had I, but at least I hadn't had my entire world ripped out from beneath me when that drunk ran a red light. I'd just had a broken heart.

"I brought a surprise," he said, giving me a shy smile.

I squinted at him. "A surprise? What kind of a surprise?"

"Hopefully a good one." He took a step to the right, revealing another young man about his age with dark curly hair, dark skin, and the most brilliant blue eyes I'd ever seen. "Marion, this is Kennedy."

"Finally," I said, moving toward Kennedy, my arms raised and ready for a hug.

He didn't miss a beat. Kennedy wrapped his arms around me and hugged me tightly. "It's nice to finally meet you Mama Marion."

I chuckled at the moniker. Ty had been calling me that ever since I'd insisted he move in with me after Trish had passed. Since he was already eighteen, he was an adult and could've done anything he wanted. And even though Trish had a substantial life insurance policy that meant he'd never have to rely on anyone to take care of him, Ty had needed emotional support and some sort of parental figure in his life. And I'd needed him, too. I needed someone to take care of while I mourned my best friend. "How long are you staying?" I asked Kennedy.

The pair of them exchanged a look that I couldn't read.

Ty's normally vibrant teal aura was now a murky green, while Kennedy's was a murky gray. It must've been part of my curse. Everything was just off, and a wave of frustration hit me. What was the point in being able to see auras if my reads were unreliable? Not that I'd ever wanted to just read auras for a living. It was the matchmaking that I was passionate about.

I raised an eyebrow and glanced between the boys. "Ty? How long is Kennedy staying?"

"Well..." He rubbed his strong jawline. "He's moving to Premonition Pointe, too. We were kind of hoping he could stay here until he finds his own place."

"Oh." That was a surprise. "Sure, I don't mind. But my dad is here, so the garage apartment is unavailable. He'll have to stay with you."

Again, another look passed between them that I couldn't parse. Was that worry I saw in Ty's expression?

But just as soon as I had that thought, Ty grinned at me and jumped up to give me a tackle hug.

I let out a small oomph, as my arms wrapped around him and then laughed at the over-the-top reaction.

"Thanks, Mar. You're the best."

"Did you really think I'd say no?" I asked, sounding incredulous even to my own ears.

He shook his head. "Not a chance in the world. But I just want you to know how much I appreciate you. Not everyone has someone they can count on to be there for them no matter what."

There was no missing the emotion that made his voice crack, and I pulled back to stare him in the eye. "Thank you. That's very sweet. But you seem..." I wasn't sure how to finish that sentence, so I settled on, "Is there something you're not telling me?"

His gaze flickered to Kennedy.

The other young man looked slightly terrified as his gaze shifted to me and then quickly back to Ty.

Ty cleared his throat, but instead of answering my question, he squeezed my hand and said, "I'm going to go help Kennedy get settled."

I watched as Ty placed his hand on Kennedy's shoulder, grabbed their suitcases, and led him toward his bedroom at the end of the hall.

Kennedy gave him a grateful smile.

There wasn't anything unusual about the interaction. It didn't take a genius to figure out that Kennedy was going through something, and Ty was doing his best to be supportive of his friend. Ty had always been the caregiver type. However, as they walked out of the living room, I got a tingling feeling at the base of my spine, and suddenly I wondered if there was something more than friendship between them.

"Damn," Celia said quietly from her spot near the entrance to the kitchen. "What is it with this joint? I swear, that damned purple light is like a disease. Is there no one in this house who isn't bathed in it?"

"Wait, what?" I asked her, my eyes wide as I stared after Ty and Kennedy. Was she implying that they were more than friends?

"My eyes hurt. I can't take it in here anymore." Celia disappeared suddenly, and I cursed under my breath.

Of all the times to disappear, why did it have to be when I had so many questions? How was she suddenly seeing love-match auras when I couldn't? But even If I'd had the opportunity to ask her about it, could I trust what she was saying? Sure, my dad and Tazia were a perfect match. I'd seen that with my own eyes a couple of nights before. But Jax and I had never had compatible auras, so that part had obviously not been true. Why would I take her word for it when it came to Ty and Kennedy? As far as I knew, Ty had never dated a guy before. He'd always had girlfriends. In fact... was he still with Camille? I hadn't seen any photos of them online recently, but that didn't mean anything either. He wasn't exactly a regular social media poster.

I shook my head. Surely Ty would tell me when or if there was something to tell. He knew I didn't have any problems with same-sex relationships. I glanced down the hall again and then went back into the kitchen to see to my guests.

CHAPTER 13

$\mathcal{I}$ found Jax, Tazia, and my dad sitting outside on my deck. That would explain why no one heard Ty and Kennedy arrive. They were discussing my lack of landscaping and apparently making a plan for a floral garden.

"Sunflowers in that corner," Tazia said. "And over there, in the shade next to the house, that's the perfect spot for a hydrangea."

"Where do the rhododendrons go?" I asked as I took a seat next to her.

She tilted her head to the side, making her curls fall over one eye. "In the front, to the left of the house. About three of them to make a foliage wall between you and your neighbor."

I nodded. "I'm going to need you to make me a landscaping plan."

"I'd be happy to, but I'll do you one better. I'll come help when it's planting season."

"If it means my gardens will look half as good as yours, I'm all in," I said.

"Don't forget the dahlias," Jax said.

My heart nearly melted. His mom had an impressive dahlia garden at their house when we were in high school, and I'd always loved it. He'd remembered.

I couldn't help the pleased smile that claimed my lips. "Yeah, I'll definitely need some dahlias. Big pink ones."

"Noted," Tazia said, gazing between me and Jax.

"You're a good friend." I squeezed her hand and then eyed her. She was wearing wide-legged linen pants and an off-the-shoulder, fitted top that made her look chic and full of style. I didn't think I'd looked that good since my midtwenties. "Tazia, what has you all dressed up today? Do you have a date or something?"

She quickly glanced at my dad and then flushed pink before looking away. "Uh, no date tonight. But I did have a lunch date today and a couple of appointments in town earlier." She straightened. "I figured it wouldn't hurt to look my best while talking to the money guys."

"You're right about that," I said with a nod, understanding now why she hadn't gone for her typical cotton skirt and peasant blouse. Her natural tendency to look like a sixties child sometimes made people not take her seriously.

My dad was starting at her, his brow furrowed. "Money guys?" he asked. "Is everything okay?"

"Oh, just fine. This was just routine stuff. Nothing to worry about." Tazia gave him a brilliant smile. "Though since I'm dressed up, we might as well not waste it. Memphis, do you have plans this evening? I thought maybe if you aren't busy, we could get out of these kids' hair and go out for a bite to eat." Tazia winked at me as if we were in cahoots on this invitation.

I bit back a grimace, knowing that was exactly what my father was going to think. That I'd played some part in getting her to invite him out. I hadn't, but did that matter so much considering I loved the idea of them dating?

My dad gave me a sharp look, confirming my suspicions that he'd think this was my idea.

"Uh... thanks, Tazia. That's a really sweet offer, but I do have plans tonight." He stood, grabbing his empty bottle of beer. "Maybe another time?"

"Sure," Tazia said without missing a beat. She stood as well and slipped her hands into her pockets. It was a tell that she was a little anxious. "I should get going." She flashed my dad a quick smile before squeezing my shoulder. "I'll see you tomorrow."

I patted her hand. "Breakfast at the Bird's Eye?"

"I wouldn't miss it." She turned on her heel and disappeared into the house. A moment later, I heard the screen door close, indicating she'd left. "Dad!" I admonished. "You do not have plans tonight. Why'd you say no?"

"Don't worry, Marionberry. I have no plans of being a third wheel with you and Jax tonight. I'm headed to the garage apartment so you guys can... do whatever you've got planned."

"You are not a third wheel," I insisted.

"He's not?" Jax asked with a barely audible chuckle.

I glared at the man sitting next to me. "You're not helping."

Jax twisted his lips into a half smile, giving me that damned dimple again. I had an intense desire to lean over and kiss it. Instead, I tore my gaze away to focus on my father's retreating form. "Ty is here."

My dad paused and glanced back at me. "He is?"

I nodded. "He just got here a few minutes ago. So as you can see, I never had plans to be alone with Jax tonight."

"Really? Maybe you should rethink that."

"Dad! You don't appreciate me interfering in your love life. Why are you sticking your nose into mine?"

Dad snorted and walked back into the house.

Jax threw his head back and laughed.

"What's so funny?"

"You and your dad. You bicker because you're exactly alike." He reached over and placed his hand over mine. "Now, about what your father said."

"You mean about us spending time together?"

"Yes." His thumb caressed the back of my hand. "Can I talk you into a walk on the beach?"

"Is that why you came by?" I asked just to avoid answering his question. Because the truth was, I desperately wanted to take an evening walk on the beach with him. But I couldn't say yes. It was such a bad idea. If we went to the beach together, I'd be breaking my personal rules. The rules that forbade me from dating Jax Williams.

"Yes," he said. "It's a nice evening, and I thought it would be nice to have company." He stood, keeping a hold on my hand as he tugged me to my feet. "Come on, Marion. It's just a walk, not a date. Just two friends getting some exercise."

"Exercise. Right. So we won't be taking a romantic walk on the beach at sunset?" I asked.

"Who said anything about romance?" He flashed his dimple at me again and started to make his way toward the house.

"Jax, wait." I planted my feet and waited for him to turn around and look at me.

"Yeah?" He had both eyebrows raised.

"It's really just a walk with an old friend? Nothing else?" I was caving, justifying the outing to myself so that I could ditch the guilt and follow him wherever he wanted to take me. If I was a stronger woman, I knew I'd see him to the door and then spend the rest of the evening regretting my decision.

"Just a walk with an old friend. Nothing more," he confirmed.

I let out a tiny sigh, nodded once, and followed him through the house. As we passed the hallway, I paused. "Hold on just a second. I'm going to let Ty know I'm heading out."

He waited patiently by the door while I strode down the hall.

Just before I knocked, I heard Kennedy's voice on the other side of the door. "You can't tell her. What if she kicks us out?"

"She would never do that, Ken," Ty said soothingly. "Marion is... Well, she's the best person I know. My second mother. She's not like your parents."

My heart swelled, and my eyes stung with unexpected tears. Hearing the love and trust in Ty's voice was a gift I'd cherish forever.

"I thought that about my parents!" Kennedy yelled. "And look what happened!"

The outburst took me by surprise, but it also knocked me out of my trance. I had no business eavesdropping on their conversation. If Ty opened the door and found me standing there, just listening, I'd want to melt right through the floor. Everyone deserved privacy. If he wanted to tell me something, he'd do it in his own time.

I backed up silently to the other end of the hall and called out, "Ty! I'm headed out for a walk. There's food in the fridge if you guys are hungry."

The door swung open. Ty was standing there with his hands in his pockets, looking somber. Kennedy had his back to both of us, and if I wasn't mistaken, it looked like he might be wiping at his eyes. There was no holding back. I knew I should've just left it alone, but I couldn't go one more minute letting him think I'd reject him, too. I walked over to Ty, took his hand in mine, and then tugged him over to Kennedy. After draping one arm around Kennedy's shoulders, I pressed a kiss to his cheek and said, "You're both perfect just the way you are, and I love you both no matter what. Understand?"

Kennedy's eyes widened in shock, and then he started to tremble as tears rolled unchecked down his face.

Ty started to reach for him, but I put my hand up and said, "Let me."

In the next moment, Kennedy was in my arms, sobbing his eyes out as I held him, standing in for the shitty parents who'd rejected him. "I'm so sorry, sweetheart," I whispered to him as I stroked a hand over his dark curls. "You're loved and welcome here, always."

He let out a sob and held on tighter. I soothed him with quiet words as he cried and then felt my heart nearly burst again when Ty stepped up behind him and wrapped his arms around both of us.

"You're safe here," Ty whispered to him. "Mom and I are here."

That was it. The tears I'd been holding back to be strong for Kennedy started to flow freely, and I clutched both of them, completely forgetting about the man waiting for me in my living room.

CHAPTER 14

*W*hen Kennedy's sobs stopped, he said, "I think I'm okay now."

Ty and I both released him, but Ty kept a supportive hand on his shoulder.

"I'm sorry," Kennedy said, wiping his eyes with the backs of his hands. "I didn't mean to break down like that."

I pressed my palm to his cheek. "You don't ever need to apologize for showing emotion in this house."

His eyes filled with tears again, but he blinked them back. "Thank you, Marion." Kennedy stared down at the floor, shifting his feet as if he couldn't wait for the moment to end.

I met Ty's eyes. "How about some hot chocolate? I'll make the good kind."

"Sure," Ty said, giving me a grateful smile as he slid his hand down Kennedy's arm and clasped his hand. "We'll be there in a minute."

I nodded and walked back into the kitchen, finding a note tacked to my refrigerator.

Raincheck on the walk? Love, J.

My heart swelled to nearly bursting. I'd completely forgotten that Jax was waiting for me, but when he realized the boys needed me, he'd quietly and graciously left without any drama, while also making sure I knew he still wanted time with me.

What was I doing, keeping this man at arms-length?

In the kitchen, I broke out the good stuff. Milk and real chocolate.

While I was busy stirring the concoction on the stove, Ty walked into the kitchen with his hands stuffed into his pockets. Without saying a word, he wrapped his arms around me and buried his head into my shoulder.

I placed my hand on his hair and just held him. There were no tears, just a quiet recognition of love between us both.

"I don't know what I'd do without you," he said when he pulled back.

"There's no need to find out." I placed my hand on his cheek and held his gaze steady with mine. "Do you want to talk about it?"

"I do, but not tonight if that's okay." He glanced behind him toward the other side of the house. "Kennedy… he's overwhelmed. I don't think he's joining us, and I don't want to leave him alone for too long."

"Of course." I pressed a kiss to his cheek. "Go on and take care of your… friend. I'll bring the hot chocolate when it's ready."

Ty gave me an amused half smile. "Boyfriend."

"I know, honey. I just wanted you to say it first." I patted his cheek. "Now go on. We'll talk tomorrow."

"Thanks," he said, his voice low and clogged with emotion. After one last hug, he left me alone in the kitchen with the hot chocolate.

Tears filled my eyes as a slow burn of rage took up residence in my chest. I would never understand how a parent could reject their child because of who they loved. The rejection that they'd rained down on Kennedy was the kind that would cause lasting trauma. I wanted to yell or scream or rip someone a new one. Instead, I stood at the stove and stirred the hot chocolate aggressively until the liquid ran smooth.

I SLEPT LATER than usual the next morning, and when I got up there was a note from Ty that he and Kennedy would be out most of the day and wanted to meet for dinner. I pressed the note to my chest, my heart swelling with affection. Trish would be so proud of him. A tiny stab of pain shot through my heart. It was so unfair that she was gone and missing seeing him turn into such a wonderful man.

"Marion?" my dad called as he stepped through the door.

"Hey, Dad," I said, stuffing the note into my pocket. I'd put it in my shoebox later with all the other notes Ty had left me over the years. "What are you up to today?"

"I have a date, so I'll be out until late." He appeared in the living room, wearing jeans and a bright blue, tropical print button-down shirt. He looked like he belonged down in Miami, not the small coastal town of Premonition Pointe.

"Date? With Tazia?" I asked hopefully.

He scoffed. "No. And don't think I don't know you're pushing that. She's not my type, so let it go."

I frowned at him. "She's your perfect type, Dad. I'm a matchmaker. A good one. When are you going to start trusting me?"

"I'm not looking for another wife. You know that." He

111

walked into the kitchen and started fiddling with my espresso machine.

"Just because you date doesn't mean you need to get married. Tazia—"

"I don't want to hear another word about Tazia! Got it?" he barked out. "I don't need my daughter pimping me out."

"Pimping you out?" I stared at him as he pushed all the wrong buttons on my machine. "Dramatic, don't you think?"

He grumbled to himself and then let out a frustrated grunt when the machine wouldn't turn on.

"I'll do it," I said with a sigh, nudging him out of the way.

He muttered something about being treated like a child but stepped aside, nonetheless.

I wielded the machine as if I were an expert barista, making us both a latte. When I handed him his mug, he nodded his appreciation before striding back through the living room. "Dad?" I called.

He paused and glanced back at me.

"Who's your date?"

"Does it matter?" he asked with one eyebrow raised.

"No. I was just curious."

He pressed his lips together into a straight line, and for a moment I was positive he wasn't going to answer. But then he stared up at the ceiling when he said, "Angela Anderson."

"Angela? Hope's mom?" I asked, unable to keep the surprise out of my tone.

"Yeah. Hope's mother. Is that a problem?"

"No." I bit my tongue, trying not to say anything, but I couldn't stop myself. "You know she reads minds, right?"

His lips twitched into a smirk. "Yes, I found that out fairly quickly. I'd say it only helped convince her to say yes."

"Oh. I see." That look on his face made me want the floor to open up and swallow me whole. I said a silent prayer of thanks to the goddess that I wasn't a mind reader, because I was certain I definitely didn't want to know how he'd charmed Angela.

Dad chuckled and waved. "See you later, Marionberry."

"Be careful!" I called after him.

He only laughed louder.

Damn him. What were the odds he'd think something questionable and Angela would kick him to the curb? Probably not all that high if Dad's insinuation was even remotely accurate.

"I HAVE THE DATABASE DONE," Iris said from her desk across from me. It was supposed to be our day off, but we'd come in anyway. We wanted to work on figuring out who might have cursed me and to try to tackle the flood of interest on the website from potential new clients.

I glanced up from my scheduling program. I'd spent the day booking appointments to meet the new clients that had expressed interest after Lennon's social media post. "Are there any people who stand out? Anyone who might have a reason to curse me?"

She frowned as she shook her head. "I did a cursory online search for everyone, and there's nothing suspicious. Do you want to take a look and see if I've missed anything?"

"Yeah. Put it in our shared folder." I stood, stretched, and walked over to the coffee maker. It was definitely a three- or four-cup day. It felt as if everything were hitting me all at once. The fire, the curse, Ty and Kennedy. Sure, I seemed fine on the surface, but the stress of the last few days was starting to get to me.

"I'll take a cup," Iris said from behind me.

I handed her a full mug and then leaned against the counter, my feet crossed at the ankles. "Did you confirm Lennon and Jax's date tonight?" As soon as the words escaped my lips, my entire body tensed and a dull ache formed over my left eye.

Iris studied me, no doubt taking in my stiff body language. "I did. They're meeting for dinner, and then will see how things progress from there."

"That's good."

"Is it?" she asked, tucking a lock of her blond hair behind one ear.

"As far as the dating agency goes, yes."

"I see." She gave me a sympathetic look and patted my arm. "I'm sure he'll let her down easy."

"I hope so."

"He will," Celia said, popping into the office suddenly. "I'll make sure of it."

"Celia, how long have you been here?" I asked her.

"Just a few minutes. I didn't want to interrupt." She smirked while flipping her hair over her shoulder.

"Uh huh. It wouldn't have anything to do with your penchant for eavesdropping, would it?"

"Penchant? Who uses that word?" Celia asked, looking incredulous. "Who are you, the Queen of England?"

Iris chuckled at the exchange.

I rolled my eyes and then stared at Celia pointedly. "I notice you avoided the question."

"What question is that?" Celia winked playfully.

"Never mind," I said, using my stern boss voice. "Just stay

away from Jax and Lennon tonight, all right? We don't spy on our clients. Ever."

"You're no fun." She pushed out her pouty lips. "What am I supposed to do then? Like you said, I'm not a great fit for the office."

"You can eavesdrop around town," Iris interjected. "See if you overhear anything that will help us figure out who cursed Marion."

Celia nodded slowly. "I can do that. In fact, it might be fun. I'll check out the gym first."

"Why the gym?" I asked, already knowing I was going to regret the answer.

"Locker room talk, obviously. Not to mention the steam room." She pumped her eyebrows suggestively. "I'm telling you, those two places are a goldmine of opportunity for information."

"I bet," I muttered.

"That's the spirit," Celia called right before she disappeared again.

"She's a handful," Iris said.

"Yes. She is." But as long as she didn't interfere with Jax and Lennon, then whatever she got up to would be fine. Besides, there wasn't anything to worry about when it came to Jax and Lennon anyway. I'd already seen with my own two eyes that they weren't the best fit. That still didn't mean I was happy about it though. I grimaced, unable to keep from picturing them together at a romantic restaurant. Jax would charm her, no doubt. And she'd flirt, making him feel good. In the end, who knew what might happen? Just because I knew they weren't a great fit, that didn't mean they wouldn't still try to date. It happened all the time… until the flame fizzled out.

Iris placed a hand on my arm and squeezed gently before dropping it. "Relationships are never easy, are they?"

"No," I agreed.

"Especially for a matchmaker who can see other people better than herself."

I narrowed my eyes at her and then just sighed. "I know what you're trying to say, but I just can't go there. It's a disaster waiting to happen."

Iris nodded. "I can see why you think that. But let me ask you this…"

After waiting a few beats for her to continue, I said, "Well?"

"Have you ever met someone whose aura was the correct match for you?" There was genuine curiosity on her face. I'd been asked that question many times over the years, usually accompanied by an undercurrent of judgment. Some clients couldn't wrap their heads around the fact that a matchmaker could be great at her job but unable to find her own match.

"Once," I admitted.

"Really?" Iris pressed her fingertips together and stared at me wide-eyed with excitement. "Do tell. What happened?"

"We were eight," I said.

"Eight years old?" she asked in a high-pitched tone, clearly shocked.

"Yep. He sat next to me in class. I was just working up the nerve to ask him to eat lunch with me when he kissed me once on the cheek and then ran away." I let out a small chuckle at the memory. "He moved a week later. It was the shortest romance in the history of Glen View Elementary."

"You lost your one true love at eight years old?" Iris asked with her hand over her heart.

"Yep." I nodded solemnly. "Pauly Baker walked out of my life forty years ago, and I've never been the same." Chuckling, I shook my head at the memory. "It's been a very long time since I thought about that."

"That's brutal," Iris said, joining me in my chuckle.

I shrugged one shoulder. "Our auras weren't a deep violet. More like a medium lavender. Which means we probably wouldn't have lasted past winter break. Too bad, too. His family had a great trampoline. I always wanted to test it out, but when the romance went south, I was out of luck."

Cackling, Iris went back to her desk and tapped on a key. After getting herself under control, she wiped at her leaking eyes and said, "Wanna start going through the database?"

"Yes." I took a seat at my own desk and said, "Let's do it."

CHAPTER 15

$\mathcal{J}$ sat on the patio at Crabby's, sipping a glass of rosé. The evening was a little chilly, but there were heaters set up around the tables. The sky was full of oranges, reds, and purples as the sun started to set over the ocean. The restaurant had started out as a favorite just because of the view, but when they added avocado fries to the menu, that's when I'd become a real fan.

From the patio, I had a view of the ocean as I sat there waiting for Ty and Kennedy, and I let the crash of the waves soothe my soul. The ocean was one of the reasons I'd chosen Premonition Pointe. This stretch of water had a calming effect on me that none of the beaches did down south. It was almost as if the water had called to me.

"Hey," Ty said softly.

I turned to find Ty and Kennedy taking seats at my table. I smiled at them. "Hey, yourself."

Kennedy nodded his greeting while Ty placed his hand over mine and squeezed lightly before removing it to pick up a menu.

I sipped my wine while they both ordered beers. Kennedy glanced over at me, obviously checking to see my reaction to their drink orders. I frowned. "Kennedy, how old are you?"

"Marion!" Ty hissed under his breath. "What are you doing?"

"Asking Kennedy a question," I said evenly. He'd been nervous with the waitress, so I figured I'd better check and make sure I wasn't contributing to the delinquency of a minor.

"Twenty-three," he said and then glanced away.

I wasn't sure why he seemed uncomfortable with that question, so I did my best to help him relax. "Ah, an older man, huh, Ty? I always found the older ones more interesting, too."

"If you call five months *older*," Ty said, rolling his eyes. But there was a small smile playing on his lips that told me he appreciated my humor.

"I... um," Kennedy stammered and then gave up as he turned his head to stare out at the water.

I watched him for a few beats and then figured it was best to just jump right in. "So..." I rubbed my hands together as if I were the evil, overbearing mom who was about to ask all sorts of personal questions and make them both uncomfortable. But before I could open my mouth to speak, I spotted a tall, very familiar man pressing his hand to the small of Lennon Love's back.

What in the hell were they doing here? I blinked and then blinked again, just to make sure my eyes weren't playing tricks on me. I was absolutely certain they had a reservation at another restaurant across town. I slipped the menu up, hiding my face and leaning into Kennedy's personal space, trying to make sure neither of them saw me.

"What's happening?" Kennedy asked.

"Those people are my clients, and I don't want them to see me," I whispered.

"Why?" Ty asked, glancing over his shoulder at them where they were seated just a few tables away.

"Because it makes it look like I'm spying on them or something." I peeked out from behind the menu and swore under my breath when my eyes met Jax's. He frowned but then smirked and shook his head slightly. I tucked my head back behind the menu and felt my face flush. "Dammit, dammit, dammit."

"Mar? Do I need to cause some sort of distraction so you can run out of here?" Ty asked, humor in his easygoing tone.

"I can do it," Celia said from right behind me, making me nearly jump right out of my chair.

"Celia!" I admonished quietly. "What are you doing here?"

"Listening in on the town, trying to get some dirt so we can find out who cursed you," she said. "What else?" She gave me a look of innocence that only proved to me that she was up to no good. Like spying on Jax and Lennon.

"You're cursed?" Ty asked, his eyes wide with alarm.

I winced. "Yes. I was going to tell you about it, but I haven't really had a chance. Just know I'm okay. Can we talk about it later?"

Ty pressed his lips together, obviously not pleased, but he nodded.

I turned to Celia and whispered, "You're doing exactly what I told you not to do!"

She snorted. "You're doing the same thing. And FYI, that menu isn't doing anything to hide you. Your hair is too big. They'd know you anywhere.

The protest was on the tip of my tongue, but when I pressed my palm to my hair, I grimaced. The evening air had taken its volume to a whole new level. I glanced at Ty and Kennedy. "Can we get out of here and go somewhere else? This is highly unprofessional. I shouldn't be here when my clients are on a date."

"Yeah, okay," Ty said, already pushing his chair back.

Before any of us could rise and head for the door, a tall blonde stomped into the building and straight over to Jax and Lennon's table.

"Bethany?" I whispered, my gaze locked on their table.

"Who's that?" Ty asked.

"Jax's neighbor." I gnawed on my fingernail, wondering if she was there to tell him his house had burned to the ground. Though since he was a volunteer firefighter, no way would that happen. His coworkers would show up en masse, all of them ready and willing to help with whatever he needed.

Bethany slammed a fist down onto Jax and Lennon's table, making their water glasses and silverware rattle. "How dare you, Jax Williams? I thought you said we were exclusive!"

I let out an audible gasp then, but no one heard me over Lennon's cry for Jax to explain and Jax's demands for Bethany to explain herself.

"I don't have to explain anything. You know what you did," she said, poking him in the chest. "We... you... I thought we had something!" Tears filled her eyes and then rolled silently down her cheeks.

I squinted, trying to see if the tears were real. After working with so many Hollywood stars, I was pretty good at spotting when someone was putting on an act. The woman's face was red, and her hands and voice were shaking. There was betrayal etched around her eyes, and something deep in my soul just said that the pain she was going through was real.

"Bethany?" Jax asked hesitantly as he reached out to touch

her arm. His face was pinched in confusion. "I... What do you mean?"

My heart was in my throat as I openly stared at the scene unfolding in front of us. Was something going on with Jax and Bethany? I'd already witnessed their compatible auras. There was no denying that they'd be drawn to each other. And the way Bethany was reacting to seeing him on a date with Lennon would have had me thoroughly convinced that they'd been lovers. But I also knew Jax. He'd always been a straight shooter. His honesty was never something I'd questioned. I'd have bet my entire career that his shock and concern wasn't an act.

"I mean..." Bethany threw up her hands and let out a cry of frustration. "You're an asshole."

Jax glanced once at Lennon, mouthed *I'm so sorry*, and then stood, reaching for Bethany. "Can we go talk for a minute?"

"Talk?" she scoffed. "That's not what you wanted to do last night, you jackass."

"*What* are you talking about?" Jax demanded.

"Don't touch me!" Bethany turned and grabbed a plate from the table next to her and threw the contents at Jax.

He quickly stepped aside, and my eyes widened in horror as I watched a plate full of linguine and red clam sauce splatter all over Lennon's white dress.

Lennon let out a cry of dismay and quickly stood, making the pasta spill from her lap onto the floor. She stood there, her arms out, palms up as she stared down at the red stains covering her body.

"Lennon!" I shot out of my chair and over to her, grabbing napkins on my way. I fruitlessly tried to wipe the excess sauce from her body but quickly gave up, realizing the only thing to do was to get her out of there. "Come with me."

"Marion?" she asked. "Why are you here?"

"I was having dinner with family," I said, glancing over at Ty and Kennedy, who were already out of their chairs, waiting to follow me. "It doesn't matter. Let's just get you taken care of."

"Marion," Jax said quietly from behind us.

I glanced over my shoulder and glared at him. "I've got Lennon. You take care of your own mess." In my heart, I wasn't sure he deserved my wrath, but if what Bethany had implied was true, that they'd slept together the night before, then he'd lied to me. He'd said he had no intention of dating her.

Sleeping together isn't dating, my mind reminded me.

Right. But that didn't mean it didn't hurt. I mentally shook myself and proceeded to steer Lennon to the patio exit so that she wouldn't have to walk through the restaurant.

"Stop!" Bethany shouted.

I glanced back, expecting her to be yelling at Jax, only her finger was pointed right at me. Or was it Lennon?

"You're a piece of work, you know that?" Bethany stalked toward us.

I glanced at Lennon. Her shock had worn off, and now there was anger burning in her bright green eyes. "You'd best step away from me," she said in a low, dangerous tone. "I don't know you, and you sure as hell don't know me. If you have a problem with your man, that's your business. Not mine. Now I'm leaving, and I suggest you get yourself under control before you get arrested."

This was a side of Lennon I hadn't actually seen before. There'd been glimpses of her strength in a couple of our interactions, but this version was a badass.

"You're right. I don't know you. I don't care either. I mean her." Bethany jabbed a finger right into my chest.

I immediately reached up and grabbed her digit and flung her hand to the side. "Hey. Don't touch me. I don't have anything to do with whatever is going on with you and Jax."

"Oh." She let out a humorless bark of laughter. "Is that what you think?"

"Bethany," Jax said again, his tone soothing this time. "Please. Can we get out of here and talk this out somewhere quieter without an audience?"

"I bet that's exactly what you want, Jax Williams. Gotta keep that nice-guy image squeaky clean, right? Well, no. I won't be pacified. We're going to have this out right here."

"Ma'am," a tall man in jeans and a button-down shirt said from behind her. "I'm the manager of this establishment, and I'm going to have to ask you to leave."

She just gave the guy a dirty look and turned her attention back to me. "You're a real piece of work, *Marion Matched*. What kind of matchmaker sets her client up with a man she knows is in love with someone else? Or strings a man along for decades, leaving him emotionally unavailable for everyone else? But he sure didn't have any problems sticking his dick—"

"That's enough!" the man behind her barked. He grabbed Bethany by the elbow and practically dragged her to the exit.

"If I were you, I'd fire Marion!" Bethany yelled, staring at Lennon. "She set you up with her boyfriend just for clicks!"

The manager stepped behind her, cutting her off from our view. Then she was gone, and the restaurant was so silent the only sound was the waves crashing from the nearby ocean.

"Is that true?" Lennon finally asked. "Is Jax your boyfriend?"

"No," Jax and I both said at the same time.

I let out a tired sigh and grimaced when I saw someone taking a photo of us. "Let's get you out of here."

Lennon noticed the table full of young twentysomethings

with their cameras out, too, and I could feel the frustration radiating off her. She turned and stalked toward the same exit that Bethany and the manager had used just a moment before.

Jax and I followed her with Ty and Kennedy remaining silent behind us.

"Well, that was exciting," Celia said as soon as we were in the parking lot. The ghost had her arms crossed over her chest, and she was glaring at Jax. It was shocking that she'd stayed silent through the entire blow-up back in the restaurant. In fact, I couldn't even remember seeing her once the commotion had started. "Jax Williams, you have some explaining to do."

Lennon, Celia, and I all stared at him.

Ty cleared his throat and touched my arm lightly. "Maybe we should just meet you back at home?"

I glanced at him and Kennedy and nodded. "I'm sorry. This was not how I'd envisioned the night going."

Ty gave me a sympathetic smile and kissed my cheek. "I can imagine." He grabbed Kennedy's hand, and the pair of them walked away, leaving us to unravel the mess Bethany had caused.

Once the boys were gone, we again turned our attention to Jax. I was the first to speak. "Are you seeing Bethany?"

"No." He crossed his arms over his chest, mirroring Celia.

"Just fucking her then?" the ghost asked.

"No!" He ran a hand through his thick curls and scowled. "Bethany is my neighbor. We're just friends. I have no idea what she was talking about."

I raised one questioning eyebrow.

"Dammit, Marion. You know me. If I had something going on with her, don't you think I'd have told you? I certainly wouldn't have asked you out if I was with her."

Lennon clicked her tongue disapprovingly. "So there *is* something between you two," she said, eyeing me and Jax.

"No," I said at the same time Jax said, "Yes."

It was my turn to glare at him. "There is nothing going on with us."

"That's not true," he said quietly, staring out at the ocean. "We both know it."

"Oh, stop this," Celia said, waving her arms. "Lennon deserves the truth." The ghost turned to my client. "Here are the facts. Jax and Marion dated a long time ago. They just reconnected and Jax wants to start something up again, but Marion doesn't think they are a good match, so she's keeping him at arm's length by setting him up with other people so she won't be tempted to go back to him. I used to think he was a decent guy, but now after the Bethany thing, I'm not so sure. So caveat emptor and all that."

"I see." Lennon's flat gaze told me everything I needed to know. She was not happy that she'd been set up with someone who was obviously interested in someone else. "I can't say this experience has been a pleasant one so far."

"I know, I'm—" I started.

She held up a hand, stopping me. "Forget the apologies. I'll do the other two dates because they are in my contract, but I will be posting about this, and don't think I'm going to hold back. If you want to terminate, then I still expect my fee and my meeting with Tandy Knight. If you don't, I'll go into the other dates with an open mind, but be warned that I'm not feeling too charitable about your services at the moment. I won't guarantee my recommendation."

Son of a fucking bitch. It was no surprise that Lennon was pissed. I would be too after that shit show. There really was no choice other than to move forward. I could not have this experience end with her posting about a date where she was assaulted with a plate of food and set up on a date with someone who was emotionally unavailable. At least I had a second and third try to turn this ship around. Everyone loved an underdog, right?

I stifled a groan and said, "I'll do my best to make this right for you, Lennon. My sincere apologies for the way the night turned out. Please send me the dry cleaning bill."

"I will," she said, turning her attention to Jax. "I hope you get whatever that was with Bethany settled. If you're being truthful, clearly you two have some communication issues."

"That's one way of putting it," Jax muttered. He held his hand out to her.

She stared at it for a beat before shaking it.

"It was a pleasure to meet you, Lennon. I'm truly sorry the evening turned out the way it did," Jax said. "I hope you find what you're looking for."

She nodded once and glanced at me before meeting his eyes again. "You too, Jax."

We watched as she walked away, and then Jax turned to me. "We need to talk."

CHAPTER 16

*J*ax and I stared at each other.

"This is awkward," Celia said. "I'll leave you two alone to... do whatever it is you're going to do." The ghost followed Lennon, whistling to herself as if she didn't have a care in the world.

Jax reached for me, but I stepped back as he said, "Marion, I—"

I held up a hand. "Save it. I don't think I want to know."

"I didn't sleep with Bethany," he said, his tone full of frustration. "I have no idea what that was back there, but none of it was true. I have never asked her out. We've only ever had drinks as friends on my porch. That's it. I wasn't lying when I said she reminds me too much of my ex-wife. I'm not interested in her."

"Then why does she think so?" I asked, not ready to just let it all go. The fact was Jax didn't owe me any explanations. His relationship with Bethany was his business. I'd turned him down and bailed on every invitation he'd extended since I'd moved to town. I had zero reason to be upset or jealous if he'd been seeing someone else.

I knew that. The problem was I couldn't shake the feeling that I'd been betrayed somehow. It wasn't fair, and I was doing my best to bury that feeling, but I wasn't being very successful.

It was also true that he'd gone out on the date with Lennon as a favor to me. He hadn't wanted to be fixed up. The poor guy was a victim in this crazy drama.

But none of that changed the fact that Bethany felt betrayed by him, and I really wanted to know why.

"I really don't know." He blew out a breath while holding the back of his neck with one hand. "Honestly, I need to go talk to her, but after that public display, I really don't want to do it alone."

I frowned, pinching my eyebrows together as I jerked back a touch. "You're saying you need an escort?"

"Yes," he said seriously. "I'm worried she's having some sort of mental breakdown. She implied we've had sex, and we haven't. I haven't had sex since…" He muttered a curse under his breath and I found myself intensely curious about that answer.

"Since when, Jax?" I asked gently. It was a personal question that I had no business asking, but he'd brought it up. How was I supposed to just let that go?

He shoved his hands into his jean's pockets. "Not since before I got divorced."

"Oh." That was a surprise. He'd been divorced for at least five years, hadn't he? And likely separated for longer than that. "That's…"

"Unfortunate?" he asked, his lips twitching in amusement.

"Very." I couldn't help it. I reached out and squeezed his hand. "Are you okay?"

"Okay that I've been celibate for far too long?"

I chuckled. "Well, that and after what happened back at the restaurant. Bethany's outburst was pretty brutal."

"I'm okay. I'm just sorry this is going to reflect badly on your dating agency." His look was so sincere, I nearly melted right there in the parking lot.

"The business will survive." I glanced around, looking for his truck. "Do you want me to follow you home?"

"My truck isn't here." He gestured to the north side of town. "Lennon and I met at Abalone for dinner, but they lost our reservation and the wait was so long we left. That's how we ended up here. She insisted on driving."

"They lost your reservation?" I asked, incredulous. "This was a date from hell."

"Pretty much. Anyway, my truck is across town."

"Looks like you need a ride." I slipped my arm through his and led him to my SUV. We were mostly silent on our way across town.

When I pulled up next to his truck, he turned to me. "Will you meet me at my house?"

"Are you sure you need me?" I asked. "I suspect you'll have an easier time getting answers from Bethany if I'm not there."

"I'm sure. I don't want you to have any doubts that I'm telling you the truth."

I opened my mouth to say that I didn't but then closed it. There was a small part of me that didn't really know what to think about the entire situation. Why would she accuse him of sleeping with her and then dating someone else if that wasn't true? Was she setting him up for something? Or had Jax turned into someone I didn't even know anymore?

That last thought hurt my heart. There was no going home. I needed answers. "Yeah. I'll meet you at your place."

Jax reached over and squeezed my leg. "Thanks."

A few minutes later, I pulled into his driveway and parked beside his truck.

His small one-story house was dark, but the porch light was on, illuminating a lush hanging garden and convertible patio set. It was truly lovely. A vision of us sitting together, sipping wine while watching the sunset, flashed in my mind. Warmth filled my chest, and I pressed a hand over my heart, wondering if that vision might ever come true.

"This way." Jax clasped my hand and led me to the white bungalow to the left of his home. A red Mustang with vanity plates that read HRS PWR sat in the driveway. "She has to be here. That's her car."

I glanced at the gorgeous vehicle and felt a twinge of envy. I'd always wanted one, but had been far too practical to pull the trigger. I admired her taste and told myself that one day I'd splurge on something like it just for me.

The porch light flicked on and Bethany walked outside. She moved down her steps as if in a trance. Her face was white and she had her arms wrapped around herself as if holding herself together.

"Bethany?" I asked. "Are you okay?"

The other woman shook her head slowly, never taking her eyes off Jax.

This was a completely different Bethany than the one I'd witnessed at the restaurant. She looked spooked and like she was ready to bolt. I didn't think it had anything to do with me. She hadn't even glanced in my direction.

"What is it? What's happened?" I asked, rushing to her side, meeting her between the two houses.

Bethany finally looked at me, her eyes glassy and full of tears.

"Come here." I guided her to Jax's front porch and sat on the couch, tugging her down until she was sitting beside me.

She didn't resist, and when she was sitting, she finally turned to look at me. "Why are you being so kind to me?"

I blinked, taken aback by her question. "Why wouldn't I be?"

"Because of the way I behaved." She was so despondent. It was a little eerie.

Jax joined us and sat on the other side of Bethany. He cleared his throat and was kind when he asked, "Why did you say all those things?"

Tears spilled down her cheeks, and she shook her head violently.

"Beth?" Jax asked again. "Please tell me what's going on. I know something isn't right. Just tell us."

She leaned her head against his shoulder, but the movement wasn't really intimate or as if it were something she did all the time. This was a broken woman who needed someone to comfort her.

I reached over and grabbed her hand, squeezing it, letting her know that no matter what happened, she wasn't alone.

She tightened her fingers around mine while also squeezing her eyes shut, and I got the feeling she was terrified.

"You're safe with us," I said, suddenly really grateful that Jax had asked me to follow him home. He'd been right. Something was terribly off with his neighbor.

"I just... I don't know what happened." She sucked in a shaky breath and sniffed.

Jax produced a handkerchief from his pocket and handed it over.

I raised my eyebrows at him. Who carried handkerchiefs these days? What was he, an eighty-year-old man?

"My dad always carried one," he explained even though I hadn't voiced my question. "I just... They're useful. I made it a habit."

I nodded at him, sort of charmed by that explanation.

"Thank you," Bethany said and blew her nose, making a honking noise that was a lot louder than expected.

"No problem," Jax muttered when she handed the used handkerchief back to him. He stuffed it in his pocket and waited.

Unable to deal with my impatience, I said, "Bethany, can you tell us how you found Jax and Lennon at Crabby's?"

She shook her head. "One minute I was cutting flowers to bring in, and the next I was parking my car at Crabby's and storming in to give everyone a piece of my mind. I don't remember changing my clothes, getting into my car, or driving over there." She turned her gaze on Jax, and with a hitch in her voice, she added, "And I have no idea why I accused you of those things. I don't think... I would never... I'm sorry. I'm so embarrassed."

Jax wrapped an arm around her shoulder and pulled her in for a side hug. His eyes met mine, and it was clear he was thinking the same thing I was. Bethany was not lying. She really didn't know what was going on. But was this some sort of mental breakdown, or...

"I think I was cursed," Bethany said. Her voice was so low I barely heard her.

"Cursed?" Jax asked, pulling away and staring down at her. "Did someone attack you? Did you see anyone while you were cutting flowers?"

"I don't think so, I..." She shook her head again. "Maybe? I saw a bike in the distance coming down the street. I thought maybe it was you." Her voice trembled. "You're always talking about getting out and taking a ride. But as the bike got closer, I realized it was only Mathew, the kid who lives down the street. I was still watching him bike closer when a tingle started at my spine. After that, I felt like I was caught in a fog, unable to control myself, but still watching myself storm into the restaurant and say all those things."

"You were deliberately trying to tank Jax's date," I offered.

"I guess, but that's not who I am. I'd never do that. It's hard to reconcile that I did." Bethany slumped back into the couch. "All those lies." She shuddered and wrapped her arms around herself.

I met Jax's gaze, and I could tell by his worried expression that he believed her. And even though I didn't know her very well, the person sitting between us wasn't the same one who'd been at the restaurant just a short time ago. Something she'd said made me uneasy. The tingle that started at her spine.

That sounded like magic.

My stomach ached. Had someone cursed her, too? "Did you see anyone besides the person on the bicycle right before the fog happened?"

Bethany turned her despondent eyes on me. She blinked twice, started to shake her head, but then stopped and said, "I didn't see anyone, but I thought I heard something. A car coming from the opposite direction. But I can't remember if I saw it or what happened to it."

I sucked in a sharp breath. "Bethany, have you ever had something like this happen before?"

She let out a bark of frustrated laughter. "You mean a break with reality? A complete freak out in front of half the town? No. Good goddess. How am I ever going to show my face in public again? I'll forever be known as the woman who went batshit over a man she wasn't even dating. Maybe I need to check myself into a psych ward."

I squeezed her hand, giving her support. "Before you jump to that conclusion, can I make a suggestion?"

"Anything," she said, slumping down further and closing her eyes. I got the impression that she just wanted to disappear.

"Can I call in the coven and have them check to see if you've been… hit with a spell that altered your thinking?" It might have been a bit of a stretch. But after being cursed, I was willing to entertain anything. It didn't make sense that this woman would have a sudden break with reality and then be perfectly fine again just a half hour later.

"You think Bethany's been cursed?" Jax said, sounding alarmed.

I shrugged. "Someone cursed me recently. I don't have any idea why either. For you, it's just a working theory. That tingling you felt and the strange way you were fine one moment, and then not, and then fine again, leads me to believe there is something suspicious going on."

Bethany got to her feet and started pacing. When she stopped, she met my gaze and said, "I'd rather be cursed than crazy. Call them."

CHAPTER 17

"*I*t's not a curse," Gigi said.

A weird sense of both relief and disappointment rushed through me. It wasn't that I wanted Bethany to be cursed, it was just that if she had been, then it would explain why she'd turned into someone she hadn't recognized.

"It was a spell that has already worn off," Gigi added, squinting at Bethany, who was still in the circle on the top of the bluff overlooking the sea.

"A spell? What kind and why?" Bethany glanced around at Gigi, Carly, and Iris. The rest of the coven had been unavailable at the last minute, but the other three had come right away. "I just don't understand why someone would spell me into becoming a delusional lunatic."

"I doubt it had much to do with you at all," Iris said thoughtfully.

I frowned. "Why do you think that?" But as soon as the words came out of my mouth, it dawned on me. "You think this is to keep targeting Lennon?"

Iris nodded. "Lennon or you."

"Me? Why me? Jax and I aren't a thing. I wasn't on the date with him."

"But you're the one who set them up," Carly added. "This could be to sabotage your business. Lennon is going to write about that date online. Everyone will know. How's that going to go over for new clients?"

"Lennon's SUV was targeted," Iris added. "Spelling someone to ruin her date could be part of that harassment. Until we find out who did it, we won't know their motivations."

"Don't Marion and Lennon both drive white SUVs?" Gigi asked. "Is it possible the person who vandalized Lennon's vehicle actually meant to target Marion and not her?"

I sucked in a breath. "That's possible." At that point, we couldn't rule anything out.

"But why did they target me?" Bethany asked as she removed herself from the center of the circle and came to sit next to me on a log. "I don't have anything to do with any of this."

I knew the answer, but wasn't willing to voice it. But it turned out I didn't have to because Gigi did it for me.

"You're friends with Jax. His neighbor." Gigi looked at Bethany, her gaze turning unfocused. "And you want to date him. It's easier to spell someone with a love spell if there's an underlying desire already there."

"Love spell?" Bethany and I said at the same time.

Gigi nodded. "This was an aggressive one. Designed to hit hard and fast. It wore off quickly because it wasn't a potion and wasn't cast with the consent of the target. Those are always likely to make the subject do unpredictable things."

"Unpredictable is one way of putting it," Bethany muttered.

She stood, her back rigid. "So, if I'm understanding this correctly, I was never the actual target of anything? I was only used as a pawn to hurt either Lennon Love or Marion?"

Gigi nodded. "That's my guess."

Bethany turned her attention to me. "Can we go? I'd really like to take a hot shower and scrub this day off me."

"Sure." I stood, thanked my friends, and told them I'd call them tomorrow.

They each hugged me and Bethany and reassured her that if anything else strange happened, she could count on them for help.

Bethany nodded stiffly, thanked them, and then stomped off toward the road.

I sighed. "This is not what I envisioned for the launch of my business."

Gigi squeezed my hands. "It's going to work out. I can feel it."

I wanted to believe her. The woman had a delicacy about her that would make the uneducated think she was sort of frail. But underneath all that, there was a strong woman who knew things. Who got strength from the ancestors who haunted her house near the sea. I held on to her words, letting them settle in my bones. Things would work out. They had to.

Jax was waiting in his truck with Bethany already sitting in the crew cab. He'd insisted on driving us but stayed back while the coven did their ritual. He hadn't wanted to be in the way. I hopped in and said, "Bethany will be fine. It was a spell, but it's already worn off."

She let out a derisive snort.

Who could blame her?

Jax nodded. "She filled me in."

I nodded once and then pressed my head to the cool window while Jax drove us back to his house.

The moment he pulled into his driveway, Bethany jumped out and started to quickly head back to her house.

"Bethany," Jax called.

She paused, turned to look at him, and then said, "Not now, Jax. I need some time… to process everything."

"Yeah. Sure." He stuffed his hands in his pockets like he always did when he seemed uncomfortable. "Just…" He shook his head. "I'm still here if you want to talk or need anything. Friends, right?"

"Friends," she said flatly and disappeared into her house.

"What was that about?" Jax asked me as he led me up the porch steps and into his house.

I sighed. "She was hit with a love spell, and Gigi said it works better on people who are already predisposed to go along with it."

Jax paused just inside his front door, his hand still on the knob. "You're saying she has a thing for me?"

Rolling my eyes, I stepped closer to him and looked up into his dark gaze. "Seriously, Jax? You didn't know?"

"I…" He shrugged. "I guess I knew that she'd probably say yes if I asked her out, but we've never been anything more than friendly."

"I told you that you're perfect for each other." I pressed my palm to his cheek. "Your auras are a match."

"I don't care about auras," he said, staring down at me, a fierceness in his gaze. "I've told you that… repeatedly."

He had. I'd always dismissed it though, believing that I knew better. After all, I'd been the one to witness relationship after relationship succeed or fail, and the odds were always in favor of those with compatible auras. "You have."

"I've also told you numerous times that I want *you*," he said, licking his lips. "Not someone with a violet aura. I want fire and passion and to *live*. Help me live, Marion. I want to feel alive with *you*."

Everything inside of me melted. All my fears, all my hesitations, the rationalizations, they disappeared. How could I keep denying myself this man? My body swayed toward him, and suddenly my hands reached up to cup his cheeks almost as if they had a will of their own.

His eyes fluttered closed as if he were savoring this moment. As if he'd been waiting a really long time for me to come to him, to finally let my guard down and show him this side of me.

"I want you, Marion." His voice was husky, full of desire, want, and need.

Tears stung my eyes, and in a halting voice, I said, "I want you, too."

There were so many emotions swirling between us. My brain had shut off and all I knew was that I had to have him. Had to surrender myself to this man who I'd been unconsciously waiting for my entire life.

Jax's lips brushed over mine softly. Just a whisper of a kiss.

It wasn't enough. Not nearly enough.

I let out a tiny, barely audible gasp as my hands moved from his cheeks. Moving one up, I buried my fingers in his hair. I moved the other one down, pressing my fingers over his rapidly beating heart.

His breath hitched and in the next moment, his lips were on mine again. There was no hesitation. Jax's arms came around me, pulling me in close as his lips claimed mine. And when his tongue dipped into my mouth, tasting me, I lost myself to him.

The world fell away. All that mattered was his tongue on mine, his hands running up and down my back, his body searing mine with his heat.

"Marion," he said softly when his lips broke away from mine and started to move across my jawline and down my neck. "I've waited so long for this. Dreamed that we'd be together again, that you'd be in my arms, in my bed, underneath me as I buried myself in you."

Heat pooled between my thighs, and I let out a moan of desire. There wasn't anything I wanted more in this world than to be wrapped in his arms again, to be taken by him, and lost in the world of passion we'd once shared.

"Come to bed with me, darlin'," he said, brushing his thumb over my fluttering pulse in my neck.

Words wouldn't form on my lips. I could only nod.

That's all it took. Jax brought his lips crashing back to mine, and as he claimed my mouth, he walked me backward toward his bedroom.

When I stumbled slightly, he didn't miss a beat. Jax just grabbed my ass and boosted me up until my legs wrapped around his waist. Then he strode into his bedroom and kicked the door closed behind him.

When he placed me on my feet beside his bed, he ran his fingers through my curls and gazed at me with such raw need that my knees nearly buckled from the anticipation. We'd barely even started, and I was ready to rip his clothes off and devour him.

That's what over twenty-five years of suppressed desire would do to a person.

Slowly, Jax ran his hands down my sides until he reached under my shirt and found the bare skin of my waist just above my hips.

A shiver rocketed through me at his touch.

"Damn," he breathed. "You're so turned on. It's making me crazy." He bent his head and sucked on my neck just below my ear and brought his hands up to cup my breasts.

I pressed into him, needing to feel more of him. To feel his entire body against mine. My hands slipped around him and when I cupped his ass, pulling him to me, he sucked harder, making sparks of desire explode through my veins.

"Dammit, Jax. I need you out of these clothes."

"Take them off then," he growled.

My hands worked fast as I undid the button of his jeans and lowered the zipper.

He didn't waste any time either. My shirt was discarded and the clasp of my bra sprang free.

Hands were everywhere as we tugged at each other's clothes and tore them off each other. It wasn't long before Jax stood before me, completely naked. My mouth watered as I took in his long, toned body. His abs rippled when I pressed my hands to his abdomen, and when one moved lower to slip around his long length, he shuddered.

"Jesus, Marion. You're going to kill me if you keep doing that."

I chuckled. "You're not eighteen anymore, Jax. I thought you'd have built up impressive stamina by now."

"Oh, I have stamina," he said. "More than you can imagine. But right now, all my teenage fantasies are coming to life again, and I'm not sure I can survive it."

I glanced down at my middle-aged body and raised one eyebrow. I was far from looking like the eighteen-year-old I'd been so many years ago.

"You're even sexier now than you were then." He cupped

DEANNA CHASE

my breasts and brought his lips down to tug at one of my nipples.

When the pleasure sent ripples of pure need straight to my sex, I no longer cared what I looked like now or then. All I wanted was Jax and everything he had to offer.

Holding his face to my breast, I threw my head back and let him work his magic tongue, and when he dropped to his knees and nudged my legs apart, I didn't hesitate.

Jax's strong hands gripped my hips, and when his tongue lapped over my most sensitive bundle of nerves, my legs trembled.

Need had taken over. Words tumbled out of my mouth. "Yes, baby. Please. Right fucking there."

Jax worked me over like a starving man, and it wasn't long before I was gasping for breath, crying out as my orgasm sent me straight into another universe. My vision blurred while my toes curled, and if he hadn't been holding me up by my hips, I was certain I would've collapsed onto his hardwood floor.

When I finally quieted, Jax lifted me and laid me gently on top of his bed. He crawled over me, placing gentle kisses from my abdomen, up my belly, over my breasts and nipples, and finally to my neck and lips. When his tongue dipped into my mouth, I tasted myself on him, and was suddenly ravenous to pleasure him, to see his eyes roll to the back of his head, to make him lose his mind as he cried out my name.

I placed a hand on his chest and gently pushed him until he was on his back, and then I lifted up to hover over the top of him. "My turn," I said, my voice husky and laced with sex.

His eyes blazed and his hand fisted in my hair. Instantly, my sex pulsed with anticipation. Jax still knew what I liked. What got me going and what turned simple desire into red hot passion. It was a language we'd spoken before and one that our bodies still understood.

I'd never had this with anyone else. The raw passion. The instant connection when we were touching each other. When we were loving each other.

"Do it, Marion. Put your tongue on me," he ordered. "I need to feel your lips around me."

I slipped my hand down and fisted his pulsing cock.

His hips jerked up at my touch, and he tightened his grip in my hair. It was the only prompt I needed to get me sliding down to do exactly what he wanted.

"Yesss," he hissed out the moment I pressed my lips to the tip of his erection.

I kissed my way up and down his velvety shaft and said, "I've missed this."

"My dick?" he asked, staring at me, the heat in his gaze nearly searing through me.

I chuckled. "Yes, but I meant this. The fire burning between us."

"You have no idea, darlin'," he said as he lifted his hips so that the tip of his cock pressed against my lips again. "No. Idea."

Staring up at him, I opened my mouth and took him as deep as I could. I held his gaze as I worked him over, listening to his moans of pleasure, his grunts of need, and his gasps when he was close. His hold on my hair tightened, nearly bringing tears to my eyes with the sting of pain, but I knew that meant he was barely holding onto control. It spurred me on.

I wrapped my hand around the base of his dick and bobbed my head up and down faster while sucking harder.

Finally, he let out a loud growl, pulled me off him, and

DEANNA CHASE

flipped me onto my back. He was on me in a second, his dick pressed right against my opening.

My entire body throbbed with need.

His eyes met mine. "Do you want this?"

"You can't tell?" I lifted my hips, making the tip of him slide inside of me.

We both groaned.

"Do I need a condom?" he asked. "I… You already know I haven't been with anyone in ages. I've been tested."

Jax and I had never used a condom before. We'd been each other's firsts. I'd been on birth control, so even though it was stupid, I hadn't even thought about it this time. "I don't want anything between us," I said. "We didn't before, and I don't want to now."

He closed his eyes and nodded, but he still didn't move.

"We're safe. I have an IUD and… Well, it's been a long time for me, too."

Jax slammed his mouth down on mine at the same time he slammed into me, driving his cock deep inside of me.

I cried out, my legs wrapping around him, pulling him in even closer.

"Fucking hell, Marion. I missed this," he gasped into my ear, and pounded into me, over and over and over again, proving that there wasn't anything wrong with his stamina. I cried out again and again, the deep, long, drawn-out orgasm consuming me.

"That's it, baby. That's it," Jax encouraged, his words coming out in short gasps. "That's my girl."

With my body wrung out and pleasure still pulsing around me, I grabbed his hair, pulled him down for a demanding kiss, and said, "Fuck me like you mean it."

Jax's eyes turned molten and he unleased himself on me, his

powerful thrusts driving deep inside of me, bringing me to the brink of orgasm one more time, until finally he buried himself in me and let out a deep moan as his body tensed above mine. Our cries mingled together in the darkness, our bodies trembling with pleasure as we crashed over the edge together.

CHAPTER 18

"*Y*ou're leaving?" Jax asked, his eyes hooded. He was lying on his bed, hands clasped behind his head as he watched me get dressed.

"I have to. Ty is expecting me and..." I blew out a breath. I shouldn't have let this happen. Not now. Not when I had so much other stuff going on. If anyone found out I'd slept with the man who'd started out the evening as Lennon's date, that was going to be a clusterfuck I couldn't undo.

"You're regretting this already, aren't you?" he said as he sat up and pulled the blankets over him, covering his gorgeous body.

"Regret? No." I walked over to him and sat on the edge of the bed, giving him a soft smile. "There's not one ounce of me that regrets what we just did."

Jax's demeanor didn't soften. "But you were going to sneak off without telling me?"

I sighed and pressed my hand to his cheek. "I was going to wake you, *after* I had my clothes on. Otherwise, the temptation... It's too great."

That got a reaction out of him. His lips twitched and his hand clutched my waist, pulling me closer to him. "I was hoping to wake up with you by my side."

Disappointment skittered through me. That was something we'd never done before, though I'd longed for it. Back in the day when we'd dated, we were both living with our parents, and even though we were of legal age, neither were lax enough to allow sleepovers. I leaned over and gave him a soft kiss. "I'd like that, too, but I have to get home to talk to Ty. I shouldn't even have stayed this long."

He raised an eyebrow at me. "Isn't Ty an adult? He's not waiting up for you, is he? Don't tell me you're not allowed to stay out all night."

I chuckled. "He is an adult, and likely he *is* waiting up for me because we have things to discuss. Things we were going to talk about at dinner before you, Lennon, and Bethany showed up and everything went to hell."

"Another time then?" Jax asked, stroking my leg.

Gooseflesh broke out over my skin. It took everything in me not to rip my clothes off and climb back into bed with him. That was why I'd snuck out of bed once he'd passed out in his after-sex haze. It was hard enough to leave after being in his arms, even harder when he was trying to coax me back into them. "Another time," I agreed and quickly stood, backing away from him.

"Marion?"

"Yeah."

"Come here."

His smoldering gaze was like a drug, and my feet moved with a will of their own until I was perched right back on the edge of his bed.

Jax reached over, buried those fingers in my hair again, and kissed me with a fierceness that left my body tingling from head to toe. When he finally released me, I was breathless and stunned into silence.

He chuckled. "Go home, Mar, before I trap you under me again."

"You're evil," I said, getting to my feet. After straightening my clothes, I glanced at him and his smug smirk one last time before stumbling back out into the night. I barely registered the evening chill. How could I when my body was still smoldering from his touch?

THE WINDOWS WERE dark when I pulled into the driveway of my house. I glanced at the clock and let out a sigh when I saw it was after midnight. How long had I been at Jax's house? Longer than I'd thought. Not that I regretted it for a moment. If Ty had gone to bed, I could always talk to him in the morning.

A pang of guilt sat heavily on my chest. There were important things going on in his life, and I hadn't exactly been completely available for him. That needed to change. Immediately. As I slipped into the house, I wished it was the old days when I'd have just knocked on his door to see if he was still awake. Usually he was. Ty wasn't a very good sleeper when there was something bothering him, and many of our most heartfelt discussions had happened in the still of the night when the rest of the world was sleeping.

I couldn't do that with Kennedy there, though. One thing I'd never do was intrude on their privacy.

After dropping my keys in the bowl near the door, I flipped the light on and let out a gasp of surprise as I jumped back and knocked the umbrella stand over. "Ty. Holy shit. You scared the hell out of me."

He was sitting at the end of the couch, a blanket tucked over his lap as he sipped from a coffee mug. "You weren't expecting me to wait up?"

"No... well, yes. But when the lights were off, I assumed you'd gone to bed." I moved through the living room and sat across from him in the oversized chair.

Ty eyed me for a minute, his gaze taking me in from head to toe. When a small knowing smile claimed his lips, I sat back in the chair and groaned.

"Stop looking at me like that," I ordered.

"Like what?" he asked innocently.

"Like you're judging me."

He chuckled. "There's nothing wrong with the walk of shame."

"Excuse me, but it's not the next morning. This isn't a walk of shame."

"If you say so." He took another sip from his mug. "There's still fresh coffee in the kitchen. Want some? I picked up a bottle of Irish cream."

"Gods, yes," I said, already rising from the chair. "I'll be right back." When I had my mug of coffee doctored, I grabbed the box of coffee cake that was sitting on the counter and rejoined Ty in the living room.

"I knew you'd bring those." He smirked and grabbed a pastry.

"You got them for me, didn't you?" I took a bite and bit back a moan when the yummy goodness hit my tongue.

"Would I have gotten it for anyone else?" he asked.

"Does Kennedy have a thing for coffee cake?"

Ty chuckled. "That's quite the opening. You can just ask

whatever you want to know about him or us. You don't have to pretend you care about his coffee cake preferences."

"We had to start somewhere," I said and took a sip of my Irish coffee.

"I guess so." Ty's teasing expression vanished as he set his mug on the side table and sat back in the couch. "If you really need to know his pastry preferences, he's a cheese Danish man."

"Really? I guess that's acceptable. It's not coffee cake, but I'll let it slide," I said with a wink, trying to keep it light. Whatever Ty wanted to tell me about his relationship with Kennedy, I wanted him to know it wasn't a big deal. Not to me. And although he certainly already knew that, I had no doubt that there was still trepidation when coming out to the parental figure in his life.

Ty rolled his eyes. "You have an unhealthy relationship with your favorite pastry."

"I know." After finishing off the coffee cake, I leaned forward, my hands together and said, "You know you can tell me anything, right? Whatever it is, it's okay."

He nodded, but took a moment before meeting my eyes. When he finally did, I was surprised to see pain shining back at me.

"Ty?" I reached out and took his hand in both of mine. "What is it? This can't just be about the fact that you're in a relationship with a guy, can it? You know I'm supportive. It doesn't matter to me who you love, only that they are kind and treat you well."

He nodded. "It's not that. I know you. I was never worried about that."

I blew out a relieved breath. For a minute there, I'd started to think I'd failed as a mother figure. The idea that Ty didn't trust me to love him unconditionally... That was unthinkable.

"Good. That's good. What is it then?"

"I'm really worried about Kennedy. His dad..." Ty shook his head and a single tear rolled down his cheek. Ty angrily brushed it away. "He lost it when Kennedy told him we were dating. He went from being the proud dad who always wanted to play golf with Kennedy to spewing slurs and kicking him out of the house."

"Bastard," I said, barely able to keep my rage tamped down. Conditional love was something I'd never understand.

Ty nodded. "That's an understatement. And worse, his mother didn't say anything at all. She just wrung her hands and watched as his dad ordered Kennedy to either 'find God' or get the hell out of his house."

"That's really awful, honey. I'm so sorry. Just in case you don't already know, he's welcome to stay for as long as he'd like. His parents are misguided at best. At worst, well, I'd rather not say."

"Thanks, Mar," Ty said, wiping at his eyes again. "It's just that prior to this, Kennedy had a good relationship with his parents. And then he told them about me and this happened. I can't help but feel like it's my fault his life has fallen apart."

"What? How could this be your fault?" I asked, not bothering to hide my astonishment. "It's not like you're blackmailing him into dating you. Wait, you're not, are you?" I teased.

"Stop. This is serious."

My heart ached for his obvious pain. "I know, love. Cracking bad jokes is just my way of trying to cope when people do the unthinkable. Why do you think it's your fault? Did you pressure him to tell them?"

"No, I'd never do that." His tone was confident and full of incredulity.

"I didn't think you would." I moved from the chair to sit next to him on the couch and then wrapped my arm around him, pulling him in so that his head rested on my shoulder. "You can't blame yourself for the way Kennedy's parents are handling his truth. That's on them. You, my lovely boy, are perfect."

He snorted. "I'm far from perfect. You just have mom blinders."

It always made my heart soar when he referred to me in any way as a mother. I'd give anything to have Trish back. There was no question about that. But in her absence, I was honored to stand in for her. "Probably. I can't help it if I think you're an amazing catch. It's what us mom types do."

"Not all moms," Kennedy said, walking in from the hallway. His hair was sticking out all over his head, and there were dark circles under his eyes.

Ty popped up and went to Kennedy's side. "Did we wake you?"

"No. I've been up for a while. When you weren't there, I started to wonder where you'd gone." Kennedy glanced at me and then the clock and then back at me. He wore a half smile when he asked, "Did my invitation to the slumber party get lost in the mail?"

I chuckled and patted the couch. "Come sit down. Both of you."

They glanced at each other and a look of amusement passed between them.

"See?" Ty said.

Kennedy nodded and smiled, making some of the exhaustion in his face fade.

"See what?" I asked, narrowing my eyes at them.

"Ty said you're this proud independent business woman who prides herself on being a self-reliant badass. But when it comes to Ty and all his friends, you can't help your mothering instincts. He said you turn to goo when someone needs you."

"Well… that's not exactly the worst thing anyone's ever said about me." I smiled at Ty, who was grinning at me.

"It's just about the most wonderful thing I've ever witnessed," Kennedy said quietly.

Ty tugged him over to the couch and gestured for him to sit next to me.

I immediately placed my hand over his and squeezed, silently giving him my support. I was starting to wonder if this young man had anyone in his life who'd loved him unconditionally. I glanced at Ty and thought, *maybe one person.* "I'm sorry, Kennedy. You deserve better than how your parents are treating you."

He just nodded once and glanced away, but not before I caught the glimmer of tears in his eyes.

"Oh, honey." I desperately wanted to wrap my arms around him, to hold him together and keep him from shattering into a million pieces. But something told me that wasn't what he needed. "You know what makes a person strong?"

"Getting knocked down and coming back up swinging?" he asked with a scoff.

"I'm guessing that's what your father told you?" One glance at Ty told me I was spot on.

"What does it matter?" Kennedy closed his eyes, and suddenly I felt as if he was shutting down, preparing to ignore everything I said. I wasn't sure how I knew, I just did.

"It matters because he's wrong, Kennedy. Real strength is being true to yourself. Living your life authentically regardless

156

of what other people think of your choices. To deny yourself that because of closed-minded people is only harming yourself. You, my gorgeous friend, deserve love. You deserve to pick the person you want to love. If that person is Ty, then don't let anyone get in your way. Not your parents, not me, and most definitely not that inner voice that is wondering if you should've just not said anything. Don't second guess your desire to live out in the open, to celebrate your love by being honest with yourself and the people you love. You deserve so much better."

"Fucking hell," Ty said under his breath as he pressed the backs of his hands to his face to stop the steady flow of tears.

Kennedy let out a surprised bark of laughter even as his own tears spilled down his face. "You can say that again."

The two gave each other small smiles before Kennedy turned to me. "I know all that. I really do. But hearing it said out loud, damn. It really touched me."

"Whatever you do, Kennedy, don't let anyone steal your happiness," I said with the utmost sincerity. "Not even your parents." I'd seen more than my share of broken people who'd been rejected by their family just because of who they loved. The trauma never really went away, but trying to conform to someone else's views was always a mistake. Even the most compatible couples rarely came back from the problems that arose when one was trying to hide who they were from the world.

"I won't," Kennedy said solemnly. Then he squeezed my hand and said, "But that means I have an opening for a mother figure. What do you say, will you be my Mama Marion, too?"

My heart nearly lurched out of my chest. "I wouldn't have it any other way."

CHAPTER 19

*S*itting at my desk, I stifled the largest yawn in history. "I think staying up past two in the morning was a huge mistake," I told Iris. After I'd done everything in my power to make sure Ty and Kennedy knew they had me on their side always, I'd filled them both in on the curse. It had taken some doing to convince Ty that I was okay and he didn't need to worry. He'd assured me that he had every right to be worried, but he reluctantly let it go when I told him the coven was busy trying to find the culprit so we could find a solution.

"What the hell were you doing up that late? Binge-watching something on Netflix? Or was it more of a Netflix and chill situation?" She smirked, clearly pleased with herself.

I nearly choked on a sip of coffee.

Her eyes widened. "It *was* a Netflix and chill situation! Spill. Who was it? It was Jax, wasn't it?"

"There was no Netflix involved," I said and turned back to my computer.

"Oh. Em. Gee!" she cried and started rambling about needing to know all of the details, but I tuned her out when I spotted the deluge of messages in my inbox. The majority were titled with NEED TO CANCEL.

"Iris," I said, my voice quiet but made of steel. "We have a problem."

She stopped chattering immediately and came to stand over my shoulder. "What is it?"

But before I could answer, she saw for herself and muttered a curse.

I clicked on the first message.

To Whom it May Concern:

I cannot work with such an unethical company and have no desire to be fixed up with a cheater. Please return my deposit ASAP.

I opened three more messages that were varying degrees of the same request. The fourth one included death threats.

"Holy shit," I said, pressing my hand to my forehead. Had someone found out about me and Jax? How was that possible? The only people who knew were Ty, Kennedy, and now Iris, though I hadn't given any of them any details.

"Oh, no." Iris pounded her fist on her desk. "What in the fresh hell was the paparazzi doing, hanging out in front of Jax's house?"

"Paparazzi?" I shot out of my chair, and this time it was me who stood over Iris's shoulder.

There I was, appearing to rush out of Jax's house just after midnight. My hair was a little wild, and I looked completely debauched with my shirt partly unbuttoned. "Son of a bitch."

"You can say that again." Iris turned to look at me. "Are you okay?"

I reread the headline.

Famed Match Maker, Marion Matched, Stole a Love Match from Social Media Client, Lennon Love.

"This will ruin us," I said.

"I'm sure we can do something to fix this," Iris said, but there wasn't any conviction in her tone.

My phone started ringing. I went to silence it but saw the name and answered. "Aunt Lucy? What's going on?"

"What's going on?" she shrieked. "Haven't you seen the headlines? You have a disaster up there, that's what's going on. What can I do? Whose kneecaps do I need to bust? I'm calling Stan. Don't worry. He'll take care of this."

"Whoa. Take a breath," I said, grinning despite the fact that everything I'd worked for was starting to crumble right out from beneath me. "Why are you calling your lawyer?"

"To send a cease and desist order, obviously. We can't have those lies about you out there unchallenged. You'd never spend the night with a client's date." There was so much conviction in her voice, it pained me to have to set her straight.

"Uh, wait just a hot second on calling Stan," I said.

"Why? Do you have a lawyer of your own? Obviously, you do. Why hadn't I thought of that?"

"Aunt Lucy, it's true. We can't send a cease and desist when they published the truth."

Silence.

I bit down on my bottom lip, waiting for her to come to terms with my confession.

"You did what?"

"I can explain. Lennon had already written off Jax and—"

"Nope. I can't hear this right now," she said. "Good goddess, Marion. Between you and your father, you two sure know how to make a mess of things, don't you? We'll talk about it tonight."

"Lucy, come on," I started, but when I didn't hear anything, not even background noise, I pulled the phone away from my ear and sighed when I realized she'd already ended the call. "Dammit. That's one more thing to add to my plate."

Iris gave me a sympathetic look and then pointed to her computer screen. "It's not all bad. Lennon just posted, and she did a pretty good job of laying out the facts without blaming the agency. Maybe that will help some?"

I quickly scanned Lennon's post. Iris was right; it could have been way worse. But it still wasn't a great look for the agency. Why would anyone trust me when I'd set up a high-profile person like Lennon with a man who appeared to have a stalker? Add in the fact that Jax and I were splashed all over the internet, and it made me and the agency look like a hot mess.

"This still isn't good," I said. "We need to do everything in our power to make sure Lennon's next date is magical."

"I'm on it!" Celia said, popping into existence right beside me.

I jumped as my heartrate spiked, making me feel as if I were going to have a heart attack. "Do you always have to do that?"

"It's part of my mystique," she said, fluffing her hair like she was some sort of fifties pin-up model.

"Mystique or not," I said, "I do not want you doing anything that interferes with Lennon's date tonight in any way. Got it?"

Celia let out a huff of frustration. "Then what am I supposed to do? I thought I was your employee. I can't do computer work, I'm not allowed to spy on people, I—"

"Wait." I held up my hand. "You're not allowed to spy on the clients. I never said anything about not spying on other people."

"Oh. Interesting," Iris said, having already figured out where I was going with this.

"Someone needs to fill me in on this one," Celia said. "Are you turning me into a private investigator or something?"

"Something like that." I pulled up the gossip site that published the article about me and Jax that morning. "See this?"

"Holy shit!" Her big eyes were like saucers when she looked at me with glee in her expression. "You did the dirty with the hunky firefighter?"

I ignored her question. "I want you to find out who did this. Are they following Lennon, or me, or Jax? Or maybe even Bethany, but I doubt it. It looks like she was just caught in the crossfire."

"So I can spy on Lennon then?" Celia asked with a mischievous grin.

I sighed heavily. "Not spy. Just see if someone is following her. Taking notes on her actions. That kind of thing."

"And you want me to do that for you, Jax, and Bethany as well?"

I nodded.

"You realize I'm just one ghost, right?" She placed her hands on her hips. "I can't be everywhere all at the same time."

"I know," I reassured her. "Just do the best you can. At least Jax and Bethany live next to each other. That should help."

"It will help when you and Jax are rolling around in the sheets, too," she said with a snicker.

A chill washed over my body." Do not, in any way, shape, or form, invade my privacy. Or anyone else's for that matter. I'll get the coven to—"

"I know, I know. Smudge my ass into oblivion. I got it," she said dramatically. "Don't be such a killjoy, Marion. A dead girl has to have some fun." She floated over to the door, but before she vanished, she glanced back at me. "Don't forget our deal. I'm still a client looking for a date."

"Do you think she'll find anything?" Iris asked.

"I have no idea, but she's sure tenacious enough. If she wants to, she will." I walked back to my computer, opened the email program, and started to process the numerous refund requests with a heavy heart.

CHAPTER 20

I sat on a bench overlooking the ocean and adjusted my large brim hat. It had been a day. After refunding eighty percent of our new clients, I called the ones who seemed open to a discussion. I'd saved only three new client contacts, who all knew me through the coven, and lost the rest.

It wasn't the week I'd been hoping for.

"I brought you something," Hope Anderson said, sitting next to me on the bench.

I lowered my sunglasses and took the small bag she held out to me. "If it's coffee cake, I think I've hit my limit."

She chuckled. "No, but I did think about it. Just open it."

I looked inside the bag and frowned in concentration as I pulled out the nondescript felted doll. "What's this? It looks like a cat toy."

Shaking her head, she sat back and laughed again. "You really do need an education on witch paraphernalia, don't you?"

I turned the doll over in my hands and although it took a

moment, it finally dawned on me that she'd brought me a voodoo doll. "Do these things work?"

She raised her hands so that they were palms up. "I don't know, but it seemed like a good idea. Mostly those kinds of curses are all about intensions, so probably? You won't know until you try it, right?"

"I don't know who I'm supposed to be torturing," I said, stuffing the doll back into the bag. "What do I do then?"

"You just need to be specific. Write down something like *the person who cursed Marion Match* and then pin it to the doll. Then when you're poking pins in its privates, that person will get a nice little surprise." She smiled sweetly at me.

I cackled. "Okay. I get it."

"I thought you'd like that." She smirked and then sobered. "That's not the only reason I asked you to meet me here."

I turned to give her my full attention. "Okay. Give it to me."

"Remember when I told you I'd listen in around town? Keep my ears open for anything that might give us a clue as to who's targeting you?"

"Yeah. Have you heard something?"

She shook her head. "Not anything more than people speculating on all the drama."

"What are they thinking?"

"Nothing you want to know." She squeezed my hand. "But my mother heard something. And her empath abilities are much stronger than mine."

"Angela overheard something?" My stomach churned with nausea. How had I gotten myself into this mess?

"She did. She said she overheard someone thinking they could get to you through your son."

"Ty?" He was the only person anyone would consider my son.

"It'd have to be him, wouldn't it?" she asked.

"Yes." My entire body went numb, but then a fire lit in my belly and that mama bear instinct came out, ready for a fight. "Whoever is doing this is going to regret the day they interfered with me and mine," I said fiercely.

Hope nodded. "Damned straight they are. And when they find out you have an entire coven behind you, they're going to be in a world of hurt."

We held each other's gazes, both of us fierce in our convictions. "Thanks, Hope. This is going to stop right this minute. I don't know how, but it is."

"Let me know what you need when you need it. I'll be there."

I nodded once at her and then stalked back across the town square, heading back to the office. But before I got to the front door, I heard my dad calling my name.

"Marion! Hold up." Dad was striding toward me, a frown on his face.

I waited, impatiently tapping my foot. I needed to get back inside to call Ty and Kennedy and warn them to be extremely careful around anyone they didn't know. "Dad, can we—"

"Memphis!" a woman called from behind him. "You can't fix this with sheer brute force. Surely you know that."

He ignored her and walked right up to me, pulling me into his arms for one of his fierce bear hugs. "Oh, Marionberry. I'm so sorry." He stepped back just as quickly and continued, "I already have my lawyer working on a retraction. By tomorrow, all of this is going to be just a bad memory."

"Dad..." I glanced at his companion. She was a slim woman with blond hair cut in long layers. Every detail of her lowcut outfit screamed money, and I suddenly wondered if she was a candidate for the next *Real Housewives* franchise.

"Hi, I'm Pixie," she said, holding her hand out. Her nails were perfectly manicured, and she had a rock the size of Gibraltar on her right hand. The diamond nearly blinded me in the afternoon sun.

"Hello," I said, politely shaking her hand. I was just about to dismiss her when I felt a tiny shock skitter over my hand. I stared at my palm and then at her.

"Static," she said with a shrug. "I think it's because of the dry weather."

Dry weather? We lived on the coast. It was never dry.

"It's because you're a spitfire, too hot to handle," my dad said, giving her a suggestive waggle of his eyebrows.

"Oh, hell," I muttered. "Listen, Dad, I have an important phone call to make. Can we talk about this later?"

"Yeah, I guess. But I'm going to need you to talk to my lawyer. I gave him your number, so don't let it go to voice mail, understand?" he asked.

"Sure. Understood," I said, watching as Pixie slipped her arm around my dad's waist and pressed her breasts into his side.

Pixie turned to me. "It was nice to meet you, Marion. I hope we get to spend lots more time together... after I show your dad a good time."

My stomach roiled, and I had to fight to keep the disgust from showing on my face. It wasn't that I begrudged my dad a girlfriend, but there was something about this woman that just wasn't right. It was a more intense version of what I felt when auras clashed, and I wondered vaguely if this was my new normal. Were my other senses kicking in now that I couldn't really read auras the way I used to?

I squinted at them, taking in Pixie's pea-green aura and my dad's pale-yellow one. Both had that tinge of brown around the edges. Nothing had changed there, but I had no doubt that these two were a terrible match. I didn't need my aura-reading ability to be working to understand that.

"Marion, did you hear me?" Pixie asked, concern radiating from her small body.

"Yeah. Sure. Nice to meet you, too, Pixie. It was a pleasure," I lied. Then I spun and hurried into my office building, only to run right smack into Jax.

CHAPTER 21

"*J*ax!" I cried as I bounced off him.

He reached out to steady me, keeping me on my feet. "Whoa. Where's the fire?"

"I have to call Ty," I said, rushing past him to my desk where I'd left my phone.

"Okay. I can wait." He walked over and sat at my desk, waiting patiently.

I didn't have time to yell at him that he shouldn't be in my office. Not after the gossip rags posted a picture of me leaving his house last night. First, I needed to make sure Ty was safe.

After quickly finding his number, I hit the button to dial. The phone rang five times and went to voice mail. "Dammit!"

I ended the call and tried again. When I got voice mail again, I left a hasty message, ordering him to call me back immediately. Then I texted him, telling him to be careful because whoever cursed me might be coming for him next and that I needed to talk to him.

My hands were shaking when I put the phone back down on the desk.

"Marion," Jax said, getting to his feet. He stood in front of me with his hands on my hips, his eyes boring into mine. "What's going on?"

"Whoever cursed me might be going after Ty, and I need to find him." I swept past Jax, heading for the door again. If Ty wasn't picking up, I'd just have to hunt him down on foot.

"Someone is going after Ty?" Jax asked.

I spun around, anger consuming me. "Yes. That's what I said. I have to go. I have to find him and Kennedy."

"I'll go with you," he said automatically and strode past me, reaching for the door.

"You can't!" I cried. "Dammit, Jax. Didn't you see the news this morning? We're all over the internet. People know we were together last night. Do you have any idea what that looks like to my potential clients?"

He frowned. "Why is it a problem if we're together?"

"You were on a date with Lennon last night!" I threw my hands up in frustration. "It looks like I stole her date."

He scoffed. "I was never going to date her. That was just a favor. And I was never supposed to be named as her date anyway."

How could he be so dense? "That all went out the window when Bethany caused a public scene. Internet sleuths figured out your identity and for some reason, the paparazzi was watching your house. Now it's out that I ended up going home with the man who cheated on Bethany to date Lennon. We both look like scum. And my business is already suffering for it. If I'm going to turn this around, I can't be seen with you. Don't you understand?"

He crossed his arms over his chest. "But none of that is true, Mar."

"I know!" I practically screamed. "But potential clients don't know that. This is a PR nightmare. I swear to the goddess, I never should've hired an influencer. There's no quicker way for a shitstorm to go viral."

Jax took a step back, shock registering on his face. "I see. I'll just go then."

I stood there in my office, watching numbly as he slipped past me and closed the door softly behind him. After a few seconds, I walked back over to my desk and threw myself into a chair.

Pure frustration consumed me, and I had to blink back tears. I'd just taken out all of my frustration and fear on the one person I wanted by my side. "Dammit, Marion. You're fucking this up," I said to myself.

But there was no time to wallow. I needed to find Ty.

Just as I was dragging myself out of my chair, my phone rang. Ty's name flashed across the screen.

"Ty?" I rushed out.

"Yeah. It's me. What's wrong?"

"Where are you?"

"Kennedy just got to the beach. We're going to take a walk. Why?"

I closed my eyes for just a minute, saying a silent prayer to the goddess that they were both safe. But that didn't mean they'd stay that way if someone was determined to curse him. "I need you to meet me at home. It's possible you're going to be the next target of whoever cursed me."

"What? Why?"

"I don't know. To get to me, I guess?"

"Okay," Ty said. "So what now?"

"Can you just meet me at home? I just need to make sure you're both okay and then we'll figure out what to do."

"Sure." He relayed the information to Kennedy, and when he spoke into the phone again, he said, "We're on our way."

Some of the tension eased from my shoulders, but I knew I wouldn't stop worrying until he was back under my roof. "I'll meet you there."

I'd just ended the call when my phone rang again. Lennon's name flashed this time.

"Lennon?"

"Marion, we have a problem," she spit out.

What now? "Please don't tell me Bethany showed up at your date again."

"No. But it's not much better. Bodhi walked out on me. We'd barely made it through the bread basket, and now he's nowhere to be found. I have to say, so far, I wouldn't recommend your service to my worst enemy."

"Bodhi just walked out? Why?" Those two were the perfect match. It's why I set them up next, because we'd all needed a win. I was certain this was a sure thing.

"I have no idea. He got up to use the restroom and never came back. We'd already ordered, so now not only do I not have a ride, I'm stuck with a two-hundred-dollar check for food I'll never eat. I'm damned sure not paying for a taxi on top of everything else. You need to come get me. Now."

My heart was screaming that I needed to get home and make sure that Ty was safe and no one had cursed him. But my head was telling me that I had to do something about the situation with Lennon. This was an epic disaster, and I couldn't leave her stranded. Once that post went viral, all of this would've been for nothing.

"I'm on my way," I said into the phone.

She rattled off the name of the restaurant and said she'd meet me out front.

Once I ended the call, I shoved the phone in my pocket and shouted, "Celia! I need you."

To my surprise, the ghost popped into existence right beside me. "You rang?"

"Were you here this entire time?" I asked, narrowing my eyes at her.

"No," she said, her mouth twisting with irritation. "You told me to watch Lennon, so that's what I was doing. When she called you, I figured you'd have questions. So I made certain to keep an ear out. But I can just go back since my presence obviously isn't appreciated."

I cursed under my breath and shook my head. "Sorry. I didn't... shit. It's been a rough day. Thank you. You were doing exactly what I wanted. But I have another problem now, and I'm hoping you'll do me a favor."

"You want me to do you a favor?" Celia asked, looking shocked. "Me? Seriously?"

"Yes. You. You're the only one who can do it. I need you to find Ty and Kennedy and stick with them until I can get there. Make sure no one suspicious gets near them. I think Ty might be the next target to be cursed."

Her eyes flashed bright with anger. "Someone is going after your Ty?"

"We think so. And I need to go get Lennon. Did you see what happened there? Why Bodhi left?"

"No, that little jackass. If I see him again, he better look out for falling limbs. Poor Lennon, she looked so dejected when she realized he was gone. It was like someone had stolen her puppy. One minute they were talking and laughing, and the next, he got up and just never returned. What kind of asshole does that to a person?"

"I have no idea. There was no indication that he didn't want to be there?" I asked, trying to reconcile why he'd just ditch her.

"None. As far as I could tell, they were having a good time. But it was hard to pay that much attention to them. Those purple auras were blinding me, and you know how I feel about purple." She mimed putting a finger down her throat and made a retching sound.

Purple auras. That meant they'd been connecting. Why in the hell had Bodhi just left? Was it some sort of long-game payback from when they'd dated before? Maybe she'd broken his heart and this was his revenge.

I'd have to see what I could pry out of Lennon... if she was still talking to me by the time I picked her up. "Thanks, Celia. Thank you for keeping an eye on Ty for me."

"No problem." She raised her hand and snapped her fingers.

The moment Celia vanished, I rushed out to my SUV and headed north.

CHAPTER 22

"*T*his is pure bullshit," Lennon said the moment I found her sitting on a bench in front of the restaurant.

An older couple who'd been walking toward the parking lot paused and glared at her.

"Listen, lady," Lennon snapped. "You'd be pissed if your date ditched you, too."

I wasn't sure if I should laugh or cry. If I were Lennon, I'd probably have lost my filter, too.

The older woman's expression turned sympathetic, and with all the sincerity in the world, she said, "Men suck donkey balls."

"Margie!" the man admonished. "That language is uncalled for."

"See?" Margie asked. "Their egos are so fragile. I say good riddance. A gorgeous girl like you doesn't need to settle for a man who doesn't respect her. I say delete his number and go get your groove on."

Lennon's eyes crinkled at the edges as she smiled at Margie.

"You know what? That sounds like a great idea. I know just the man, too."

"Good for you," Margie said and walked off with her head held high, her date trailing after her.

"You have a man in mind already?" I asked Lennon, my eyebrows shooting straight up. Surely she wasn't talking about Jax, was she? My stomach ached at the thought.

"Sure. Who doesn't want to get together with a musician? Bain's the perfect rebound guy." She shrugged. "How do you think that will go over on social media? Girl ditched, so she falls into bed with a hot guitarist. If the fling lasts even a few weeks, I'm sure it will be good enough to bring you some clients. Everyone has a musician fantasy, right?"

Lennon had undoubtedly been going for a light tone, but there was a distinct bitterness beneath the surface. No matter how much she wanted to hide it, she couldn't fool me. Bodhi had hurt her... deeply.

It was clear to me that she didn't want anyone to see that vulnerable side though, so I followed her lead. "You know what they say; the fastest way to get over someone is to get under someone else. I'm sure Bain would be an excellent candidate."

"I don't need to get over him. It's not like I was in love with Bodhi."

"Right. I get that," I said, glancing around the parking lot, wondering if there was any chance that Bodhi hadn't left yet. I just couldn't understand why he'd ditch her. "I just meant that if Bain's who you want, then you should go for it."

"Yeah," she said flatly. "What do I have to lose?" She stalked over to my SUV, yanked the door open, and climbed in.

I followed her. We were mostly silent on our way back to town. She only spoke when she directed me to her short-term rental. "No word from the police about who vandalized your car?"

"They're still going through the camera footage," she said, staring at the unassuming cabin that overlooked the sea. "They're supposed to get back to me in a few days. I figure after tomorrow's date, I'll move back home."

That startled me. "Are you sure that's safe?"

Lennon turned to assess me. "Do you know something I don't?"

"No, I..." Dammit. This was the moment of truth. I hadn't told her I'd been cursed. That was something I'd wanted to keep close to the vest. But I couldn't let her go on thinking the vandalism was the only thing that had happened. Not if it would put her in danger. "Yes."

Lennon didn't say anything, just waited for me to continue.

"It appears I was cursed the night of the mixer." Clutching the steering wheel, I stared out the windshield, trying to control the anger that had started to consume me. "The curse has messed up my aura-reading abilities. I have no idea why I was targeted. No idea who did it. Only that it happened, and now someone out there is trying to get to me through my son."

More silence. It was so quiet in the car I was almost convinced that Lennon wasn't even there. That she'd slipped out and I hadn't even noticed.

Finally she cleared her throat.

I glanced at her.

She was staring pointedly at me. "Your SUV looks a lot like mine."

I knew where she was going with this. "Yes. It does."

"That means that vandalism might have been meant for you, and that I wasn't the target at all."

"It's possible." I nodded. "But I can't be sure, since we don't have any leads at the moment."

"Is there a reason you didn't tell me this?" Her tone was cool but not angry.

I let out a huff of humorless laughter. "A number of them." It was time to be real with Lennon Love. "But the biggest one is because I have put practically everything I have into opening Miss Matched here in Premonition Pointe, and I need my business to be successful. I didn't want anyone to know that my abilities have been compromised. It would be detrimental to my livelihood. But also, I wasn't sure that you hadn't been targeted, so it was best that you stay vigilant for your own safety."

Lennon's expression was unreadable, and I was certain that I'd just sunk my dating agency. When she posted about this, that would be the death knoll.

But when she spoke, she completely took me off guard. The confident diva I'd come to know turned into someone else completely. "That's really devastating, Marion. I'm so sorry you're going through this." She glanced down at her hands in her lap and said, "I wouldn't have told me either." When she raised her gaze to mine there was a glint of amusement there. "You never really can know what someone like me might post. Those of us who are used to living our lives out in the open sometimes don't understand boundaries."

I was shocked into silence at her understanding and humility.

"I very much doubt that your aura-reading ability is the only reason you're successful as a matchmaker," she continued. "Throughout this entire disaster, you've been here for me without complaint. And for that I thank you. I think a lesser person might have thrown their hands up and demanded that I never post about what's happened. They'd threaten to withhold my fee or any number of things. But you've been fair, and because of that, I won't mention any of this. If you still want to continue of course. You seem to have a lot on your plate at the moment."

It took me a minute to compile my thoughts. Was this kind, caring woman the same one I'd been dealing with the last few days? Sure, she hadn't been awful, but she had been a diva and a little prickly. This was a side of her I hadn't witnessed before. "I do have a lot on my plate, but your date with Bain is already set up for tomorrow. You're going to the beach for a surf lesson, right?"

She nodded. "It's something he does regularly, and I've always wanted to try it, so we're meeting in the morning at Premonition Cove."

"Then keep the date. There's really no reason why you shouldn't, unless you're just fed up, too. I won't hold you to anything. I know this has been a disaster. I swear to the goddess, this has never happened before. I've had people go on dates that weren't quite right, but those didn't include jealous outbursts or a man walking out on a date with zero warning." I pressed my fingertips to my temple. "In fact, I don't think I've ever had a client walk out of a date like that with no warning. It's very unusual."

"It figures everything would go sideways when the entire internet is watching, doesn't it?" It was Lennon's turn to let out a humorless laugh. "Maybe it's me. Maybe I'm the curse. I certainly haven't ever had any success at dating. That would explain everything."

I shook my head and gave her a small smile. "Everyone thinks that when they are navigating the dating waters. For what it's worth, I'll do everything in my power to find you someone great, even if you strike out three times. We don't have to post about it. In fact, it's probably better if we don't. Perhaps the *Bachelorette* style of advertising we've been doing is working against you."

"Maybe," she said, looking sad. "We'll see how it goes. I might need a break after this to regroup."

"I understand." I gave her a sympathetic smile.

She returned my smile and said, "I'm going to go in and eat a pint of ice cream." She grimaced as she glanced down at her body. "Maybe only half a pint if I'm going to squeeze into that wetsuit tomorrow."

I chuckled. "Sounds like a plan."

"Thanks for coming to get me, Marion." She opened the door. "I really do hope everything works out for you."

"You're welcome. And thanks." I waited in the driveway until she was safely inside and then hurried home to make sure Ty and Kennedy had made it back safely.

CHAPTER 23

"Ty!" I called as I pulled my front door open.

"In here!" he called, sputtering through laughter.

My anxiety immediately eased at the cheerful noises coming from my living room. I walked in prepared to fine Ty and Kennedy, but instead Aunt Lucy was standing in the middle of the room with a plastic device in one hand and a zucchini in the other.

"I'm telling you, guys, if the equipment ever fails to inflate, just get yourselves one of these bad boys and you'll be in business in no time." She proceeded to place the plastic device over the zucchini and then started squeezing a small attached ball. "See? It squeezes at the base of your... ahem, member, and gets the job done."

"Aunt Lucy! What in the world are you doing?" I cried. The words flew out of my mouth even though it was obvious she was giving a demonstration on how to use a penis pump.

"Oh, Marion. There you are." She dropped the equipment

and the zucchini and rushed over to me, pulling me into a tight hug. "I missed my girl," she said into my ear.

I hugged her back, holding on tightly. "I missed you to. What are you doing here, besides giving a sex ed talk to Ty and Kennedy?"

She pulled back and giggled. "They were curious. What else was I going to do? Send them to YouTube?"

"Uh, yeah. That's what I would've done," I said, feeling my face heat. I was hardly a prude, but walking in on my aunt, who was in her seventies, giving a penis pump demonstration to the man I thought of as a son was a little much, even for me.

"Why in the world would I do that?" She looked genuinely perplexed.

"Because…" I shook my head. "I have no idea. Where did that come from anyway?"

"Oh, it's your father's. I—"

"Dad's?" I waved my hands in front of my face and backed up, making Ty and Kennedy fall out with laughter again. "This is too much. I can't… why in the world would you have that?" I asked her.

"I picked it up from Candy, of course. That troublemaker was still flashing it around the internet like a complete lunatic. I swear. You'd think she'd have a smidge of decency."

"You're one to talk." I waved at the device. "If it's Dad's… oh gods." I closed my eyes, trying not to picture *anything*. "Why is it out on the table, and why in the world would you touch your *brother's* penis pump?"

Ty was laughing so hard that he was curled up on the end of the couch, his hand on his stomach, and tears rolling down his face. Kennedy wasn't holding it together much better as he gasped for air.

Aunt Lucy shook her head. "Don't be so dramatic, Marion. It's not like the outside had been contaminated."

The front door opened and heavy footsteps sounded on my floors. A moment later, Dad walked in. "Looks like there's a party going on."

"A sex party," Ty gasped out.

"What?" Dad glanced around, looking confused. Then his gaze landed on his sister and he added, "Lucy! When did you get here?"

"About a half hour ago." She walked over and hugged him.

Lucy had been down in LA visiting friends for the past couple of months while her house was being remodeled. In fact, I was pretty certain the construction wasn't even completed yet. I glanced around, wondering where she was going to sleep, and decided the only option was my room. It looked like I'd be on the couch. Just a perfect ending to a shit-show day.

"How was the drive?" he asked her.

"It would have been better if I'd had company. You know, if you would've told me you were coming up here, I'd have come with you," she said, her tone stern. "I don't know why you're always going off half-cocked like that."

"Half-cocked," Kennedy wheezed. "Oh, man. I'm dying."

I couldn't help it. It was too much. Laughter bubbled out from the back of my throat, and I joined the boys in their fits of hilarity.

"What's gotten into them?" Memphis asked.

Lucy just smiled and waved at the penis pump on the coffee table.

Dad's eyes widened when he spotted the device. Then he frowned. "Lucy, why did you bring sex toys to Marion's house?" His eyes widened some more as he quickly glanced around the room. "I thought Ty was joking about there being a sex party."

His words only brought more laughter, and I collapsed into a chair, completely unable to contain myself.

"Of course there is no sex party, Memphis." Lucy clucked her tongue. "Do you think I'd attend a sex party with my brother and my niece? Come on now. That sort of thing is reserved for when I'm with my swinger friends." She winked at Ty and Kennedy, signaling she was just putting them on. "I was just showing the boys how to use the penis pump in case they ever have a need for it. Do you have any tips?"

"Tips!" Kennedy and Ty said at the same time and then gave each other high fives.

Dad rolled his eyes at Lucy. "You always were a troublemaker. And no, I don't have any *tips* for the penis pump. It's not something I've had a use for," he said with a sniff.

"Really? It's nothing to be ashamed of," Lucy said casually. "I've had men use them, and I gotta say, it really helped." She smiled sweetly at him.

"That is not anything I need to know," he said, turning on his heel. "I think I'm going to bow out before this conversation gets any weirder."

"Wait," Lucy called as she scooped up the pump and tossed it into a cardboard box before picking the entire thing up and handing it to him. "These are yours. I got them from Candy so she'd stop spreading bullshit about you all over the internet."

Dad held onto the box, frowning in bewilderment. "You what?" He scanned the box. "None of this stuff is mine."

Lucy raised a skeptical eyebrow. "None of it? Not even the sweatpants?"

He carefully pushed the penis pump aside and pulled out a

pair of gray sweatpants. There was a redwood tree patch on the back over a pocket.

"Still not yours?" Lucy asked.

"You know they are. Okay, the sweatpants are mine. The rest? This... device, the video tape..." He visibly shuddered. "The nudie magazines, these are *not* mine."

Lucy eyed the cover of the porn magazine and nodded. "Yeah, you never did prefer the really skinny ones. You always bought the ones with ample cleavage."

Dad ran a hand down his face as he groaned. "Lucy, for the love of everything sacred, would you please not talk about my... *any* of this when I'm in the room. It's disturbing."

"Don't worry, darling brother. Even if the penis pump wasn't yours, you have one now. It will help if anything I say causes you performance issues."

"Jesus," he muttered. "How do I get myself into these things? Damned Candy. I knew I should've stayed away from her. Why do I always attract the crazy ones?"

"That's easy," Lucy said flippantly. "It's because you aren't discerning. As long as a woman shows interest, but not too much interest, you'll date her. It's not hard to end up with a batshit crazy woman when you don't have standards."

"I have standards," he said, sounding annoyed.

"No you don't," I chimed in, backing up my aunt. "You don't even date one woman at a time. It's like a revolving door."

"That's not true," he said. "Candy and I were exclusive for a few months."

"Yesterday you were on a date with Angela and today you were running around with that Pixie woman. She was acting like you two were headed for a chapel in Vegas."

"We are not headed for a chapel in Vegas or anywhere else,"

he said, sounding horrified. "And what's wrong with dating around?"

"Nothing," I said, feeling a little bad that Lucy and I had ganged up on him.

"That's right. There's nothing wrong with playing the field. I'm not hurting anyone. I don't see the problem. And frankly, it's really none of your business," he told me. Then he turned to Lucy. "Or yours. So butt out."

All the laughter had died out as we watched him storm out of the room, leaving the offending box behind.

"Well, that was a party killer," Lucy said. She linked her arm through mine. "Don't worry about it, sweetie. He'll get over it."

I was sure he would, but was it really fair for me to judge his dating choices just because I wanted him to be settled down with someone like Tazia? I honestly thought he'd be happier with someone like her, but it wasn't my call. And it wasn't fair to push him into something he wasn't ready for. "I should apologize to him."

"We'll do it together," she said.

I glanced at Ty and Kennedy. "Did anything unusual happen today?"

"Only when Celia showed up and started asking us if we knew any dead guys she could date," Kennedy said with a smirk. "I told her my cousin passed away last year, but that he's gay, so I didn't think he'd be interested."

"That didn't stop her from asking Kennedy if he'd participate in a summoning ritual though," Ty said with a grin.

My stomach started to ache again. A summoning ritual was the last thing we needed at the moment. With my luck, they'd summon a demon. "What did you say?" I asked Kennedy.

"I told her that Ricky and I hadn't been speaking when he passed, so it was unlikely he'd answer my summons. He stole my boyfriend, so I got revenge by replacing all his underwear with granny panties. He had to wear them in the locker room, and you can imagine how that turned out."

"Why didn't he just go commando?" Ty asked.

Kennedy shrugged. "He was a little insecure when it came to the size department." He smirked and then his expression turned sad. "We didn't talk for six months, and then the car accident happened. Honestly, I'm not sure I'd have ever forgiven him for what he did, going behind my back with Brian, but I still miss him."

"I'm sure you do," Ty said sympathetically.

"Anyway," Kennedy said, seemingly brushing off his melancholy "after we got home and Lucy showed up, Celia said she had other people to watch over and vanished into thin air."

I nodded. "That's good." It meant she was keeping an eye on Lennon, Bethany, and Jax.

Ty yawned, and a few moments later, he and Kennedy headed for bed.

I held my arm out for Lucy. It was time to sooth my father's ruffled feathers. "Ready to eat crow?"

"There's no time like the present," she said, and together we went to apologize to my dad.

CHAPTER 24

*A*fter leaving the garage apartment properly chastised by my father, Lucy and I started to make our way back to the house.

"That could've gone worse," Aunt Lucy said.

"You think so?" I gave her a disbelieving look. "He ordered us out of the apartment and told me if I mentioned his dating life again, he was going to cut me out of his will."

She waved an unconcerned hand. "Please. He's just embarrassed about the penis pump. You know how sensitive men are about those kinds of things."

"He might have a point about me butting in too much," I said, my shoulders hunched. "I just know he'd be perfect with Tazia, but instead, he always chooses the ones who never last."

"That's because that's what he wants, sweetie. He's protecting his heart. Surely you know that," she said gently.

"I do. I just want better for him."

"I know." She slipped her arm through mine. "So do I." We started up the steps to my cottage when she said, "Who's truck is that?"

I followed her gaze and sheepishly replied, "Jax's."

"Does this mean what I think it means?" she asked, eyeing me suspiciously.

"That there's something going on with us? Yes. So you need to call off your lawyer about that retraction because it's true that I was with him last night. We don't have a leg to stand on. Free press and all that."

"I see." She tapped her finger to her lips and shrugged. "I'll let him work on it anyway. There's no reason why your private business should be spread all over the internet. At the very least, he'll make them think twice about publishing anything gossipy about you again. No one likes when lawyers get pushy."

I hugged her. "You're the best. You know that, right?"

"I do what I can."

Once we were inside, she kissed me on the cheek and said, "I'll give you some privacy. Just let me know when you're done and I'll make myself comfy on the couch."

"No way. You take my room," I insisted. "I'll take the couch."

"Marion," she started, but I cut her off.

"I insist. No arguments. I won't have my aunt on my lumpy couch even for one night."

She pressed her lips together as if she was gearing up to protest, but then she nodded once. "Okay, fine. But tomorrow I'll find somewhere else to crash until my house is done."

I'd fight her on that, too, but for the time being, I just nodded and said goodnight.

I found Jax in my kitchen, sitting at the table with a mug of coffee in front of him. When he spotted me, he didn't say anything. He just sat there watching me. I walked over to the coffee maker, poured my own cup, and went to sit next to him.

"Are you here to tell me last night was a mistake?" I asked.

"Is that what you want me to say?" His voice was gruff with a hint of irritation.

"No," I admitted.

He turned to me, eyes searching. "What are we doing, Marion?"

"I honestly don't know," I said, turning my attention to the coffee mug. "But earlier today... I owe you an apology. I should not have taken my frustrations out on you."

"Okay." He blew out a breath. "Thank you for that. I know things are stressful for you right now. I wish there was something I could do to help."

I nodded toward the other room. "Wanna find a way to speed up the remodel on Aunt Lucy's house? Because it appears she's sleeping in my room until it's done."

He frowned. "Are they behind in the work?"

"Yes. About a month."

"I'll see what I can do."

"Seriously?" Jax was a general contractor, although his company built new houses and rarely did renovations on existing homes.

"Sure." He smiled at me. "If she'd come to me first, I'd have put her on the schedule."

"But you don't do kitchen and bath remodels," I said.

"Not usually, but for Aunt Lucy I'd have made an exception. I'll stop by and check on things. If I can help in any way, I'll let you know."

I placed my hand over his and squeezed. He was such a good man. Why couldn't he have been my perfect match?

A little voice in my head said, *he still could be.*

Jax turned his hand over so that it was palm up. I slipped my fingers through his and just held on.

"I know you're doing everything you can to get your

business up and running and that the article doesn't help with perception. If you want me to lay low for a while, I can do that for you. But, Marion, you have to know I'm not giving up on this. On us. I don't care what your aura reading says or doesn't say. I know in here that we have something special." He touched his free hand to his heart. "Don't you believe in free will? Haven't you told me before that people without matching auras make their relationships work?"

"Yes. That's true," I said softly. "But I think—"

"No buts, dammit. Why are you always trying to sabotage what we have? You did it when I went off to college, and you're doing it now before we even have a chance."

Had I been the one to sabotage our relationship back then? I frowned and bit down on my bottom lip. I remembered him leaving. It had been brutally hard for me. We'd decided to date other people and then when he finally did, I'd been crushed. "You're the one who started dating someone else. I don't see how that was me sabotaging anything," I said defensively.

He scoffed. "You're the one who wanted us to date other people. I didn't. Before I left, you told me numerous times that we couldn't hold each other back. That I had to explore and make sure my perfect match wasn't waiting for me. I didn't want that. Don't you remember that?"

Yeah. I remembered. "We both decided that was the right way to handle it. Being eighteen, how could we know what the future would bring?"

"I knew what I wanted," he said, his gaze boring into mine. "You insisted. Multiple times. I only agreed because you wouldn't let it go. You said we had to be free to explore other people or we wouldn't make it. I thought that meant you were breaking up with me. And even then, I never had any intention of dating anyone else. It was only after you told me you were dating Sean Caster that I finally agreed to a double date to help a buddy out."

I sat back in my chair, stunned. "Sean Caster?"

"Yeah," he spit out. "Sean Caster. You told me you two had started dating. That was when I finally decided to take you at your word and started seeing people. After that, we didn't talk much."

I sat there, stunned. The name Sean Caster sounded familiar to me, but I hadn't dated him. He was just a guy who I'd worked with at a café. Had I really told Jax I was dating him? Had I blocked that out? The name was really specific. "I… holy hell, Jax."

"What?"

I shook my head. "I never dated Sean. I think I must've told you that so that you'd start dating other people."

"You what?" He jerked back, making the chair squeak on the hardwood floor. "Why? Why would you do that, Marion?"

"Because I thought I was holding you back, I guess." That *did* sound like something I'd do. I had always believed that there was someone perfect waiting for him. That person had been his ex-wife. Only they hadn't been perfect together, had they? They'd broken up for some reason.

"Son of a bitch! Will you ever stop believing you know what I want better than I do?"

His words hit me like a sucker punch to the gut. He was right. Back then and even now I was convinced that there was someone better waiting for him. Someone who could make him happier than I could. And I was always doing my best to push him away, even though it tore me apart when I did it. "I'm sorry, Jax. I never meant to hurt you."

"Yeah, well, you did. More than you know."

I glanced over at him, tears stinging my eyes. "I think…" I

sniffed. "I know this has everything to do with my parents. They weren't a good fit, and I always knew they wouldn't make it. I just never wanted that to be us. For us to hurt each other so much. I guess I thought if I didn't give us a fighting chance, then we'd never end up like them. Fighting all the time. Staying together because of me. And then later, my mom finally leaving when she thought she'd finished her job of raising me." I pressed my face into my hands. "My dad is still messed up about it. You have to see it. He never dates anyone who'd be good for him. Only people who are content with short-term flings."

"That really bothers you, doesn't it?" he asked gently. "That your father never looks for someone he can be happy with, right?"

"Yes." I dropped my hands and met his gaze. There was understanding there but also determination.

"Don't you see that's exactly what you do, Marion? You don't let me in because you're afraid you'll get hurt."

"I'm not afraid for me, Jax. I'm afraid for you. I just want you to live a happy life, one you deserve, and I'm not sure I'm the one who can give it to you."

There. It was all out on the table now. It had never been about me. If it had been, I'd have never let him go. I just loved him too much to put him through a relationship like the one my parents had.

"How about you let me worry about me for a change," he said softly and wrapped his arm around my shoulders, pulling me into him. "And maybe you can find it in your heart to let me love you the way I've always wanted to."

My insides melted as emotion overwhelmed me. I pressed my head into his shoulder and let the tears fall. "I've wanted that for a long time. I was just too afraid to let myself believe it was possible."

Jax pressed his lips to my forehead and stroked his hand down my arm. "It's possible, darlin'. Trust me. It's possible."

My heart broke wide open and finally, after all those years and distance we'd had between us, I let go of my long-held belief that Jax and I could never be anything more than friends. I lifted my head, staring up at him through teary lashes and said, "Okay. I'm ready to try."

"Thank the gods," he said and kissed me.

We sat at the table for a little while longer, and then Jax led me to my couch. We laid down together with me wrapped around him, and finally after all those years, we slept an entire night together.

CHAPTER 25

I woke to someone clearing their throat. Squinting up through the morning sunlight, I spotted Ty staring down at me, an amused expression on his face.

"Morning," he said.

I jerked upright and accidentally delivered a blow to Jax's gut.

His eyes flew open as he let out a grunt of pain. "Ouch. That's a hell of a way to wake up your boyfriend."

"Boyfriend?" Ty and I said at the same time.

Jax glared at me. "I thought we settled that last night?"

"We said we'd start dating, but I didn't know we were going with labels already," I said, running a hand over my messy curls.

"Well, now you know," Jax said, sitting up and wincing when the aches and pains from sleeping on a cramped couch caught up with him.

Jax glanced at Ty. "Hello again." He held out his hand. "I'm not sure we've formally met. I'm Jax Williams, Marion's boyfriend."

Ty laughed and clasped his hand. "Ty Kirkwood. Marion's…" He looked at me for clarification.

"I took in Ty after my best friend Trish passed away," I said. "While it's not official, I consider him my adopted son."

"Yeah, son works," Ty said with a wide smile.

Kennedy walked into the room and paused when he saw the three of us making introductions.

"And this," Ty said, "is Kennedy Christian, my boyfriend."

Both boys stiffened while they waited for Jax's reply. But I knew there was nothing to worry about and was not surprised when he smiled at Ty's boyfriend. "Nice to meet you, Kennedy."

The air in the room changed, and everyone seemed to relax.

Jax rose from the couch. "Who wants breakfast?"

"I do," Aunt Lucy said from the hallway. She glanced from me to Jax and then back to me again. "Having a good morning?"

"Yes," I said simply and followed Jax into the kitchen. He quickly pulled me into his arms.

"It's not exactly how I envisioned waking up with you in my arms, but it could've been worse." Jax smiled and brushed a light kiss over my lips.

I chuckled. "Sure. I could've decked you instead of just elbowing you in the gut."

"Let's skip that and try to aim for something a little less violent and a little more… sensual." His lips traveled down my neck, and all I wanted to do was pulled him into my bedroom. But with a house full of people, there was no way that was going to happen.

"Ahh," Aunt Lucy said. "I remember mornings like that. What I wouldn't give for a hot piece of a—"

"Aunt Lucy!" I cried as I stepped back from Jax. "I think we get the picture."

"I'm sure you do." She winked and headed straight for the coffee maker.

Jax laughed and the two of them started to plan breakfast while I excused myself to change my clothes and get ready for the day.

The rest of the morning was spent around the breakfast table enjoying waffles, sausage, and bacon as the people I loved most chatted happily, telling stories mostly about me. The only person missing was my dad.

I kept glancing toward the front of the house, hoping he'd finally make his way in. When eleven o'clock rolled around, I finally gave in and went to the apartment looking for him only to find it dark with morning dishes in the sink. Sighing, I trudged back to the house and was met on the front porch by Ty, who was holding my phone in his hand.

"It keeps blowing up," he said. "I think someone wants to talk to you."

"Thanks." Five missed calls, all of them from Iris. She was covering the office this morning and I was due in later in the day. The phone flashed her number again, and I immediately answered it. "Iris, what's wrong?"

"We have a big problem." She sounded hurried, like she was rushing around.

"About?"

"It's Bodhi Bliss. He's missing. No one has seen or heard from him since before his date with Lennon last night. I tried to get in touch with Lennon, but she's still on her date with Bain and isn't answering. Do you know if she and Bodhi actually met up?"

"Yes," I said, pacing my front walk. "He picked her up and

they went to dinner at a place twenty miles north of town, but then he ditched her in the middle of dinner. Went to the restroom and never came back."

"Holy hell," Iris said. "His roommate, KC, called this morning. Said Bodhi never came home last night. He said he didn't think anything of it until Bodhi didn't show up for his niece's soccer game this morning."

"Missing a soccer game hardly sounds like an emergency. Maybe he went to a bar and hooked up with someone and just forgot," I said.

"He's the coach, Marion. KC says he lives for those games. That he never misses them. I'm telling you, this roommate of his is freaked out."

"Do you have his number?" I asked. "I want to call and talk to this KC myself."

"Yeah. Texting it to you now."

"Thanks. I'll call you back." The moment I ended my call with Iris, I called KC.

"Yeah?" he said by way of greeting.

"KC? This is Marion Matched from Miss Matched Midlife Dating Agency. I'm calling—"

"Have you found Bodhi?" he asked, cutting me off.

"No. I just heard that you think he's missing, and I was hoping to get more information from you."

The door opened and Jax walked out onto the porch, giving me a concerned look. I put my hand up, indicating that I'd talk to him when I had a chance.

"What information? He left to go on his date with Lennon and never came back. Now he's not at Lindy's soccer game, and I'm worried. He never misses Lindy's games. They are sacred. I mean, he'd be more likely to miss his own wedding than to miss one of her games."

"That's pretty serious," I conceded. "Okay, then maybe you can help me out a bit. When's the last time you saw him?"

"I don't know. Like right before he went to pick up Lennon. Six maybe? Why? When did Lennon last see him? Do you know? Have you spoken to her? Is he still at her house? I know Lennon's important to him and all, but I still don't think he'd ditch Lindy's game just for a third or fourth round of sex."

I cleared my throat. "Um, Bodhi didn't stay over at Lennon's last night, KC. In fact, he left midway through dinner."

"What?" He sounded genuinely shocked. "No effing way. Bodhi would never do that. Do you know how long he's been waiting for this second chance?"

That was news to me. It had been pure luck that he'd even been invited to the mixer. I'd found him online and sent him an invitation when I realized he was her ex, because who didn't love a second-chance romance? My heart fluttered as I looked over at Jax.

"Listen, Marion," KC said. "I don't have any idea what's going on, but I know two things: Bodhi loves his niece more than anything and soccer is sacred. He also has been in love with Lennon for two decades, and the only thing that would make him leave her at dinner is if aliens abducted him. If he left, it's because someone forced him to. Understand?"

I was starting to. Lennon had said the date was going great. She'd been shocked when she'd found herself sitting alone when he didn't come back from the restroom. And now KC was talking about how Bodhi was missing and had been waiting for his second chance with Lennon for years. My skin started to tingle, and my head swam. "KC?"

"Yeah?"

"Can you meet me at the Premonition Pointe coven circle?"

"Why?"

"I'm going to do everything in my power to get my friends to execute a finding spell. I think you're right."

"Right about what?" he asked, sounding confused.

"That the only way Bodhi would've left was if he was abducted. We can't waste any time."

"Yeah, I can do that. I'll be there."

"Great," I said as the head fog cleared. "Bring something important to him. Like a favorite watch or cufflinks. Something he wears or is likely to keep on his person."

"I'm on it. See you in thirty."

After we disconnected, I immediately called Iris and filled her in. She quickly offered to call the coven members and said she'd see me soon.

Jax was already off the porch and by my side when I shoved the phone in my pocket. "Need some help?"

"Yes." I pressed my hand to his cheek. "I have to go meet the coven. Will you stay with Ty, Kennedy, and Lucy? Make sure no one curses any of them."

He blinked at me twice then nodded. "Of course. I'll keep your family safe for you."

I threw my arms around his neck, hugged him fiercely, and said, "I'll be back as soon as I can." After grabbing my keys, I ran out to my car. Once inside, I yelled for Celia, but for once the ghost was nowhere to be found. I just had to pray that she was still watching over Lennon.

CHAPTER 26

$\mathcal{T}$he cool mid-morning breeze chilled my skin as I sat in the middle of the coven circle, voodoo doll in my hands, waiting for the coven to arrive. It hadn't taken me long to get to the bluff overlooking the water, and instead of waiting in my SUV, I'd grabbed the voodoo doll that had still been in the backseat and went to wait.

I'd thought Hope was slightly off her rocker when she'd suggested the nondescript doll, but now I was all in. Completely on board and ready to do some damage. I was well aware it probably wouldn't do anything, especially since my witch powers were mostly relegated to reading auras, but it still made me feel better to stab the doll with the safety pin I'd found at the bottom of the satchel I carried with me everywhere.

"Take that, you twisted piece of dog turd," I snarled as I stabbed the doll's legs right where the knees would be. When the doll barely moved, I jabbed twice more before moving on to his abdomen. That was a lot more satisfying, watching the doll's body flex as if it were cringing every time I jabbed it with the safety pin. "You deserve way worse," I told the doll. "Something more like this might be appropriate." With rage surging through my veins, I picked up the doll and wrapped one hand around its small neck and started to squeeze.

I imagined its eyes going wide and then popping out altogether as it clawed at the unbreakable vice cutting off blood flow to the brain.

"Marion?" a man called, and I immediately dropped the doll, feeling foolish.

"Yeah?" I stood up, turning my back to the ocean as I spotted a handsome man, probably in his early forties with wavy salt and pepper hair that was a little too long and covering one eye. He wore holey jeans and a faded T-shirt. To say he looked like a middle-aged surfer was an understatement. "KC?"

He nodded.

"I'm glad you're here. I'm just waiting for the coven, and they should be here any minute."

"All right." He dug into his back pocket and pulled out a small silver-framed picture. He handed it to me. "It's not something Bodhi wore, but he kept it by his bedside all these years."

I took the photo and had to blink back tears when I realized it was a picture of Bodhi and Lennon when they were much younger. He had his arm draped over her shoulder, and she was gazing at him like he was the only thing in the world. It was both touching and heartbreaking, because that could've been me and Jax. How many years had we all wasted, trying to figure ourselves out before finally making our way back to the ones we loved?

"This is perfect. Thanks."

"We're here," Iris called as she and the other five coven members all rushed to the circle together.

"That was excellent timing," I said.

Iris nodded. "We all pretty much pulled up at the same time. I assume you're KC," Iris said, walking over to the man who was just staring at all of us, looking dumbfounded.

He cleared his throat. "Um, yeah. You're all witches?"

"That's the rumor," Grace said as she got to work on the salt circle.

The coven moved quickly, setting up the candles and a bowl of herbs. Joy plucked the picture from me, studied it for a moment, and then shook her head. "No visions. Unfortunately."

I let out a sigh. That wasn't unexpected. Her visions were rare, but it would've been nice if this could've been easy.

"What is it? What went wrong?" KC asked, staring at me.

"Nothing. They're getting ready to start." We both turned to see the coven line up in their regular circle. This time Joy took the lead, belting out the chants that made the candles rise in the air. Before long, she was sprinkling the herbs over the picture frame. Sparks burst from the candles as they rose impressively, putting on the normal display.

KC clutched at my arm. "Whoa. This is intense."

Was it? To me it looked like just another ritual. It was then I decided I'd spent too much time with my witch friends. When floating candles and sparks of energy barely fazed me, I knew I'd been desensitized to the awesome display of power my friends shared.

Their chanting intensified, the candles went out with a whoosh, and smoke filled the air in front of them. Everyone was completely silent as they turned to look at where I was standing. I frowned at them. "What?"

Iris blinked. "Marion, you're glowing."

"Huh?" I glanced down at myself, finding white light enveloping me. Only then did I sense the magic tingling over my skin. "I don't understand. Why is this happening?"

"Our spell is calling to you. You need to walk into the circle," Joy said. She waved a hand, indicating that I should cross the salt circle and join them.

"Um, is this safe?" I asked, though I wasn't sure why. It certainly wasn't the first time I'd been a part of their circle.

"Of course it is," Carly said gently. "Come on in. Let's find out what this is all about."

Nervous, I swallowed the lump in my throat and gingerly crossed into the circle. Immediately, the smoke from the candles coalesced and then parted as if opening a window. Images began to flicker, moving too quickly for me to make anything out. I was trying to keep up, but then suddenly, the flashing stopped and showed an image of a lake that I recognized. And off to the left was a portion of a cabin that I knew all too well.

I let out a gasp. "That's my father's fishing cabin at Lake Pointe."

Joy gave me a wide smile. "I think we've just found Bodhi."

"What? No way. He can't be out there. Why in the world would he be at my dad's fishing cabin?"

"There's only one way to find out," Iris said. "She fished her keys out of her front pocket. "I'll drive." She grabbed my arm and tugged me along with her back toward the cars.

"Iris?" I asked. "Is that bad? That I'm the one who saw where Bodhi is?"

"Not necessarily," she said. "But it doesn't look good for your dad. Was he home last night when Lennon and Bodhi were out on their date?"

"I'm not sure," I admitted. "He came into the house after I got home, but I don't know how long he'd been in the apartment before that."

"Where's your dad now?" she asked.

"No idea. But Dad didn't have anything to do with this. Why would he abduct Bodhi? That makes no sense. I don't think Dad even knows who he is."

"You're right. It makes no sense," she said. "Now we have to go find out what's going on. Maybe it's just that Bodhi's at the lake. The cabin was only partially in the vision, right?"

I nodded and sent a text to Jax, letting him know we were on our way to the lake, but to stay put with Ty and Kennedy. I'd let him know if we needed anything. He texted back a protest, but when I stressed that Ty might be a target and that I had the entire coven, he relented.

Once we were in Iris's car, I glanced back to see KC climbing into his truck and following us.

"Dammit. I forgot all about him," I said.

Iris glanced in the rearview mirror and gave me a half shrug. "It's not a bad thing to have a little muscle around, right?"

"Right," I said and then worried my hands all the way to the lake.

Once we got close, Iris parked her car a quarter of a mile away from my dad's cabin.

"I figure it's best not to announce our arrival," she said.

"Agreed."

Just as we were ready to take a look around, KC arrived and jumped out of his truck. "I'm going with you."

Iris and I glanced at each other and then nodded.

"Iris is in charge, got it? She's the witch here." Just as I said the words, the rest of the coven showed up and piled out of a large SUV.

"Are we ready to find our man?" Hope asked.

"It would appear so." I looked around the clearing. "Why don't we split up? Iris and I will check my dad's cabin. Grace, Joy, and Hope, check the property to the east, and Carly and Gigi the one to the west."

They all quickly agreed and then we split into three groups. I went straight for the path that I knew led to the lake front. It was better than walking down the road right by the cabin. Iris and KC followed, all of us silent. I wasn't sure what we were expecting to happen. It was a cool late January morning. None of the neighbors appeared to be around, and everything was still. Even the air.

But as we got closer to the lake, I started to feel more and more uneasy. My skin itched, and my head started to ache. "Is anyone else starting to feel a little off?"

"No, I'm okay," Iris said.

"Same," KC added.

Maybe the feeling was because of the remnants of the finding spell. After all, I was the one who'd been affected and had seen the lake and cabin. I took a deep breath, trying to fortify myself, and forged on. We came out of the foliage near the lake. Nothing appeared to be out of place. There wasn't even a boat on the water. I glanced at the cabin. No lights were on, and the porch was void of any life. No shoes. No fishing gear. No chairs to signify someone was staying there.

"We better check the cabin," I said.

Neither Iris nor KC contradicted me, so I took off in that direction. But as soon as we started to move that way, my headache cleared and my skin no longer itched. It was then I knew we were headed in the wrong direction. We had to go back toward the lake. I turned and just kept moving toward the energy that was rapidly making me feel like I was walking through magical sludge.

"This is starting to feel a little creepy," Iris said.

"It is?" KC asked, sounding confused.

"Do you feel that magic, Iris?" I asked her.

"Yes. Only it's not the good kind."

"Nope," I agreed. "I hope you have some tricks up your sleeve if we run into anyone casting spells."

"I have a few," she reassured me.

But it didn't. Not really. Not when I didn't have anything to defend myself. Well, nothing but a few years of self-defense training anyway.

"This way," I said, instinct taking over. I led us over a small wooden bridge and then suddenly stopped and pointed downward. "There. He's under there."

KC didn't hesitate. He jumped down into the stream, glanced around, and then let out a growl before disappearing under the bridge. A few seconds later, he reappeared with Bodhi over his shoulder in a fireman's carry. Once they were back up on the bridge, KC put Bodhi on his feet. Bodhi wobbled a little, but he clutched KC's arm and managed to find his balance.

"Oh my goddess," I gasped out. He really had been under there. "Are you okay, Bodhi? What happened? How did you get here?"

He groaned and pressed a hand to his head. "I have no idea. Just... can you get me out of here? KC, take me home."

"Sure, brother. Come on."

We headed back toward the cars, but on the way, I spotted a woman out in front of the cabin. She was stalking toward us, seemingly following some sort of trail, but when she spotted me, she froze.

"Pixie?" I called. "Is that you?" It was the woman my dad had been with the day before. "Is Dad here, too?" Her makeup was smeared, and her hair resembled a bird's nest. She was a far cry from the put-together woman I'd met less than twenty-four hours earlier.

"Um, yeah. But he's sleeping." She glanced back at the cabin and bit her lip. "He didn't have a great night last night."

Because he was mad at me and Aunt Lucy. But I didn't tell her that. "Did you two come up to do some fishing?"

She ran a hand through her hair but winced at the movement and pressed her hand to her abdomen. She sucked in a few shallow breaths to get her breathing in order and then nodded. "Fishing, right. Always a good time."

I glanced again at the porch, noting none of my dad's equipment was there. When I glanced back again, Pixie was smoothing her shirt down, but not before I noted the red rash-like marks on her stomach. My gaze automatically dropped to her knees, and I saw the same small, pinprick rash.

Suddenly everything clicked into place as I recognized those same areas that I'd tortured on the voodoo doll. I pointed at her. "You! You're the one whose been doing all this to me. But why? And why did you abduct Bodhi?"

"I have no idea what you're talking about," she said primly, her head held high. "I'm sure your father won't like those accusations either."

Guilt and doubt slammed into me. If I was wrong and accused his current girlfriend of being a lunatic, he really would disown me.

"Why do I feel like I know her?" Bodhi asked no one in particular. Then suddenly he straightened. "You're the one who asked for directions when I was leaving the restroom. And then... I don't remember anything." He frowned. "You did this to me?"

"I... no," she stammered.

"Yes, I think you did," Bodhi said, his anger making him stronger. "You drugged me and then pushed me off that bridge."

"Stop it!" she ordered him, and Bodhi's mouth instantly clamped shut.

Her smile was a twisted version of the cat that ate the canary. "Now come back to me. We still have work to do."

"No way in hell, lady. Bodhi's going home with me," KC said, keeping a tight hold on his friend's arm.

Pixie rolled her eyes. "You homosexuals, always so dramatic. He can go home with you when our work here is done."

"We're not gay," KC said, glaring at her. "And again, no. He's not going anywhere with you. Go fuck yourself."

I had to admit, I liked KC's style.

"He will!" She aimed her fingers at Bodhi, magic sparking, but before she could fire, Iris blasted her with a bolt of magic that sent her flying back ten feet. Her eyes widened in shock, and then when she hit the ground, her expression turned to a mix of anger and pain.

Iris walked over to her. "I think you owe us an explanation."

"Go suck a dick," Pixie ordered, sounding bitter and annoyed at the same time.

"Maybe later," Iris said in a casual tone. "But not before you tell us why Bodhi was under that bridge and why you're determined to take him back with you."

Pixie glared at me. "He was going to make your little advertising campaign the success of the century. I couldn't have that, could I? And if he goes back to that tart of a social media whore, this will have all been for nothing."

"What do you mean, all for nothing?" I asked, stalking toward her. That itchy feeling was back, and my head started to fog slightly. Only this time I was able to control it better.

"I don't have to tell you anything," she spat. "Why didn't you just leave town when I warned you? No one wants you here!"

"You mean you're the one who vandalized Lennon's car? Only you meant that message for me, didn't you? You cursed me!" I shouted, astonished. Why was this older woman so hellbent on ruining me and running me out of town? Had she caught wind that I didn't like her dating my father? That couldn't be it. I'd just met her the day before.

"Everyone drives the same damned car these days. How was I supposed to know the difference?" she asked.

At least Lennon was safe. No one was actually trying to come for her. That was a relief.

"Pixie, I don't know what beef you have with me, but it ends here. You're going to lift this curse, you understand?" I asked forcefully. "This witch right here, she's going to make sure of that. And trust me, you don't want to be on the receiving end of her wrath."

"I don't?" She gave me a twisted little grin, snapped her fingers, and sent an electric bolt of current through the air. All of my friends dropped instantly, including KC and Bodhi.

I gaped at her. "What in the hell did you just do?"

"Get Bodhi. Let's go," she ordered me. "We have business to discuss."

"No she doesn't!" Kennedy cried just before he tackled Pixie and then zip tied both her hands and feet together. Ty came up from behind Kennedy with a piece of Duct tape, ready to secure it to Pixie's mouth.

"Just one second," I said, stopping Ty as I crouched down to talk to the woman. "Why were you targeting me?"

She let out a low growl of irritation. "You are a piece of work, Marion Matched. You're the reason I'm divorced. My husband came to you, looking for someone half my age. Do you know how long it took him to leave after you matched him with his little tart? Two days. After fifteen years, we ended in two days."

I narrowed my eyes at her. "I don't match married men. Ever. I have no idea what you're talking about."

"We were never legally married. Just common law. But we made promises, and then you came along. You're a menace to every woman in a committed relationship. You need to be stopped." There were tears streaming down her face, and all I could think was that she looked broken. She was the picture of severe mental health issues.

"I did nothing to you," I said flatly. "But you took away my ability to read auras. And you're going to reverse that curse. Mark my words; you will never be rid of me until you do."

"Eat shit," she spat.

I knew then it was a lost cause. Unless the Magical Task Force made her reverse this curse, she wasn't even going to entertain the idea.

Ty shook his head and put the Duct tape over her mouth. Then he came over and hugged me with everything he had. "When I saw her spewing that toxic magic, I was so worried about you. But then Kennedy..." Ty shook his head. "What a badass."

I had to agree and gave Kennedy a long hug, the kind I reserved for those I loved most in the world. When I pulled back, I frowned and asked, "Not that I'm complaining, but what are you two doing here?"

They glanced at each other, and then Ty said, "Your dad called. She had him tied up in there."

"In the cabin?" I asked.

"Yep. It appears someone was prepping for a little bondage when Pixie went off the deep end," Ty explained. "She tied him up and put him in the closet. Told him she'd only let him out once you were out of their hair."

"Oh my gods!" I cried. "How did he get in touch with you if he was tied up?"

Ty shook his head. "Turns out, she's an idiot and somehow kicked the cordless phone in there. He could only remember the house number by memory, so he called until we picked up. I tried to call you, but I'm guessing you don't have your phone on you?"

I patted my pockets. "Shit. I guess not. It's probably in the car." I eyed the cabin again. "So my dad is still in there?"

Ty nodded.

"Is he decent?"

"Yes," Ty said with a huff of laughter. "Jax is with him. He's just a little…"

"Embarrassed?" I supplied, pleased that Jax was watching over my dad.

"No, well yes, but freaked out is more like it. He just kept mumbling something about crazy bitches and that he was through with them."

"Goddess above, I hope so." I glanced down at the bound and gagged woman and wanted to kick her. Instead, I consoled myself that I still had that voodoo doll, and that Miss Pixie was likely to get a punch in the crotch later. The evil bitch.

It wasn't long before the rest of the coven showed up and offered to stay with Pixie while they waited for the Magical Task Force to arrive and take her into custody. This time when

Iris called, they said an agent would be on his way shortly. They didn't take kindly to witches using magic to abduct people.

"Thank you," I said to Iris as I pulled her in for a hug. "I owe you."

"No you don't. But you're welcome." She kissed me on the cheek. "Now go get your dad and Bodhi out of here. We'll make sure the task force has the numbers they need for statements."

"You're the best." I instructed Bodhi, KC, Ty, and Kennedy to head for the vehicles. With any luck, me, Jax, and my father would be following shortly.

CHAPTER 27

"*D*ad!" I called as I walked into his cabin.

A groan came from the kitchen.

I found him sitting at the table with his head in his hands. "Don't say it. I know. I know! I date the worst women."

Jax appeared and put a glass of water in front of him. "I'll wait outside for you two."

I gave Jax a grateful smile and squeezed his hand as he walked by. Once Jax was gone, I placed a hand on dad's shoulder and squeezed lightly as I said, "I wasn't going to say that at all. It turns out that Pixie targeted you to get to me."

"What?" He dropped his hands to look up at me. "Why?"

"I fixed her ex up with the love of his life, and she blames me for their breakup."

Dad frowned at me. "You don't match married men."

"That's what I said." I gave him a small smile. "They weren't married. I had no idea he was involved with someone." I shrugged. "Maybe they weren't even together really and she just went off the deep end. Who knows? But she's the Magical Task Force's problem now."

"She's the one who cursed you?" Dad asked.

"Yeah. She's not going to reverse it either. I'm sure I'll have to wait until hell freezes over before the Magical Task Force will entertain the idea of helping me."

"We'll find a way, Marionberry," Dad said and covered my hand with his. "Ready to get out of here?"

"More than you can imagine," I said.

He chuckled humorlessly. "I think you're underestimating how much *I* want to get out of here."

"Fair enough." I slipped my arm through his and added, "She didn't try to put a penis pump on you, did she?"

He glanced down at me, a stern expression on his face. "That's not funny."

"It's kinda funny," I teased.

"Your aunt is going to pay for this," he grumbled.

I laughed then sobered. "Seriously, Dad. Are you okay? Do we need to go get you checked out at the hospital?"

"I'm fine. All she did was tie me up, naked, and put me in the closet. It's fine."

I shuddered just thinking about it. No one wanted that vision of their parent in their head.

He cackled again and then we went outside, collected Jax, who was sitting on one of the steps, and headed back to where the cars were parked. Iris was there, still busy cleaning up the mess with Pixie, so dad and I caught a ride with Ty, Jax, and Kennedy after I retrieved my phone from Iris's car. On the way back to town, Bodhi called from KC's phone and wanted to know where Lennon was. I immediately gave him the name of the beach where she and Bain were.

"Good. I'm on my way," he said and ended the call.

I turned to Ty. "Head to the beach. I need to see this reunion."

Ty didn't hesitate, and we ended up pulling in right behind KC and Bodhi.

Bodhi jumped out immediately and started running toward the beach. The five of us piled out of the car, and I'd just started to slowly make my way down the beach with Jax by my side when I heard screaming.

Jax stood behind me, his hands on my waist as we watched a woman waving her arms and pointing out into the waves as she shouted, "She's hurt! She needs help. Someone help her!"

Bain, the musician, was standing at the edge of the ocean, staring helplessly at the pounding waves.

"It's Lennon Love!" someone cried out. "She's caught in a wave cycle. They keep crashing down on her."

"Lennon!" Bodhi cried as he threw himself into the water and started swimming out toward her.

"Oh my god," Jax whispered in my ear. I could only nod my agreement. What we were watching was horrifying. Lennon was in real trouble.

"Fuck!" KC cried and followed his friend.

The two men sluiced through the water like it was their day job and were just about to reach Lennon when Celia suddenly appeared, reached into the water, and yanked Lennon up by the life vest. Lennon was just bobbing there on top of the waves when Bodhi reached her. He quickly got an arm around her neck and swam as fast as he could to outrun the next wave. KC joined them and together, the two men brought Lennon back to the beach safely.

The small crowd that had gathered on the beach cheered, and it wasn't long before they all started chanting, "Bodhi! Bodhi! Bodhi!"

"That's crap," Celia said, sounding very put out. She was

hovering near me now with her arms crossed over her petite body. "I'm the one who saved her ass."

"You did," I said, smiling at her. "I saw you."

"So did I," Jax agreed. "Very impressive."

"Thank you! At least someone appreciates my talents. I can't wait for this to go up on social media. *Matchmaking Ghost Saves Social Media Star!* Kind of catchy, right?"

"Sure. But the story is going to be about her first love saving her right before they get engaged." I nodded to where they were down on the beach. Bodhi was down on one knee, clearly pouring his heart out to her.

"Oh, dammit! Can't a ghost ever get a break? Or a date for that matter?"

"It's a tough break, Celia, but thank you anyway. You watched over Lennon, and I really appreciate it," I said.

Celia's eyes misted with tears. "Did Marion Matched just thank me? Did she really just give me a compliment?"

"She did," I said with a chuckle.

"Well, that's something, I guess." She wiped at her eyes before saying, "I can't watch this anymore. Bellow if you need me." Then she was gone.

Jax and I turned to Ty, Kennedy, and Dad. "Ready?" I asked.

"More than ready," my dad said, already hightailing it to the car. Something told me all he wanted to do was hole up in his apartment for the next week and regroup. I could hardly blame him.

When Jax fell behind to talk to Ty, Kennedy slipped his arm over my shoulders and smiled at me. "You're like the coolest mom I know."

I snickered. "Maybe that's cause I'm not a real mom."

"Oh, you're real all right," Kennedy said seriously. "And I'm not the only one who thinks so." He nodded to Ty. "That one loves you like a mother, and I know we haven't known each other long, but I'm pretty sure I will too."

My heart melted. "What an incredible honor it would be for you to love me like a mother. Thank you for that, Kennedy. You boys mean the world to me."

"Are you buttering her up?" Ty asked Kennedy suspiciously.

"No,' Kennedy said, sounding offended.

"I think you are," Ty said, giving me a smirk.

"Okay, what is it?" I demanded. "What exactly do you think you need to butter me up for?"

"You'll see," Ty said.

TY DIDN'T LIE. As soon as we walked into the house, I knew exactly what that conversation about buttering me up had been about. The little fluff ball ran right up to me and wagged its tail wildly while jumping up on my leg for attention.

While my heart melted instantly, I jerked my head up with as stern a face as I could muster and asked, "Whose idea was this?"

Ty and Kennedy both took a step back, and I mentally patted myself on the back for not instantly caving.

"Ty? Was it you?"

Jax chuckled. "You guys are in deep shit now."

No one answered Jax.

Ty shook his head, denying culpability for the puppy, but then just as quickly, he nodded and scooped the puppy up into his arms. The puppy instantly started laying kisses all over his face. Ty laughed. "Chill out, girl. We're supposed to be making a good first impression. You don't want to end up homeless in less than twenty-four hours, do you?"

The puppy only wagged her tail faster and then started nipping at Ty's face.

I laughed. "Goddess above. What have you sent to my house and why?"

"Marion!" Aunt Lucy came running into the room. Her hair was frazzled and she looked a little rumpled, which was unusual for her.

I glanced past her shoulder and asked, "Do you have company?"

"What? No." Then she stared at the puppy. "Unless you mean Paris here. She's been running me ragged the last few hours. Who knew that Yorkies had so much energy?"

"Paris?" I asked, one eyebrow raised. "Please tell me her last name isn't a hotel franchise." Jax chuckled, making me smile. It was hard to be stern when my boyfriend was amused by the boys' antics.

Ty laughed. "No, but I considered it. We named her Paris Francine because Kennedy and I had our first date in Paris last year when we went to the film festival."

"That's adorable." I reached out and took the puppy, holding her close to my chest. "Now, tell me how Paris ended up in my house, and who exactly is going to take care of her?"

They glanced at each other, and I thought Ty would explain, but it was Kennedy who took over. "I have a friend down south who committed to adopting her over a month ago. Then he got transferred out of the country, so she needed a home. I said I'd always wanted a Yorkie, and he said, fine. She's yours. He just wanted her to have a good home, I guess. We were going to ask how you felt about having a dog here while we're crashing, but we wanted to ask you when things calmed down."

Ty put his arm around Kennedy and continued. "Our plans were changed when Paul, that's Kennedy's friend, called to tell us he was coming through town this morning and was going to drop her off. We had about forty-five minutes to get ready for her."

"How could you say no to this widdle-bitty, cutie-patootie pie?" Lucy asked in the most annoying baby voice ever.

"Stop," I told her and turned my body so she could no longer be crowding the puppy with her face.

"Yes, stop," Jax agreed with a grimace.

"You're not going to kick her out, are you?" Lucy asked, sounding horrified.

"Of course not. Gods above. Who do you think I am?"

They all grinned, including Jax, and I knew I'd been had. But honestly, I didn't even care. The puppy was adorable, and Ty and Kennedy looked so happy. That was all that mattered.

"My only rules are that you're completely responsible for housebreaking and cleaning up any accidents. She's your dog, so behave as if no one else is here to care for her unless you ask first. No assuming someone will let her out and then getting surprised when she piddles on the hardwood. Got it?"

"Got it!" The boys said in unison.

"The last rule is that I get to love on her whenever I want."

Ty snorted. "Sure, Mama Marion. Anything you want."

I held the puppy up, touching nose to nose, and said, "Did you hear that, Paris? I'm Mama Marion, but I'll answer to anything as long as there are puppy kisses involved."

Jax laughed as he came up behind me and slipped an arm around my waist. "I told them you were a sucker for the kisses." He kissed my neck, and right then, even after the shittiest week ever, I was happier than I'd ever been. My dad was home safe. Lucy was back in town and as sassy as ever. I had Ty and Kennedy and the sweetest puppy I'd ever met. And Jax, the love of my life. I didn't know where we went from here, but for the first time in my life, I was ready to find out.

CHAPTER 28

"This looks amazing." I turned around in a circle, taking in Aunt Lucy's new kitchen. Three months ago, it had been an L shape with dark brown cabinets, yellow laminate counters, and a brown and yellow linoleum floor. I'd teased Lucy that it was like an eighties time capsule. The new cabinets were white shaker with stainless steel hardware. I ran my hand over the new gray quartz counters and admired the farmhouse sink.

"The wood floors are my favorite," Lucy said, beaming. "They're hand scraped you know."

I chuckled. "Yes, I do believe you told us that already." It was sweet how excited she was. Two weeks ago, when Jax had stopped by, the contractor told him they were running out of money and out of time. If Lucy wanted them to finish, they'd need another infusion of cash. Cash she didn't have.

After Jax threatened them with lawsuits and complaints to the licensing board for trying to take advantage of an older woman, they'd changed their tune pretty quickly. After that, Jax had stopped by almost daily to check on their progress and to make sure they weren't cutting corners. I suspected he'd had his crew over once to install the floors since they went from being scheduled six weeks out to suddenly going in overnight. And the bill had been substantially lower, but so far he was playing innocent.

"I'm moving back in today," Lucy said. "And your dad is coming with me."

"He is?" I glanced over at my father. He was standing at the back door, admiring the new landscaping.

"Yep. He said it's time to get out of your hair and asked if he could rent a room. Seems he's moving here permanently."

I eyed my dad, wondering what was really going on with him. Ever since the day Pixie had locked him in the closet, he'd been subdued. He'd been hanging around my house, spending time in my garden, and reading a lot. He hadn't gone out on one date. I'd tried to broach the subject with him, but he'd shut me down pretty quickly. I'd let it go after that.

"He didn't say anything," I said, still watching him.

"I'm sure he'll get around to it soon, sweetie."

"Yeah." But when? As he was walking out the door? I wasn't sure why it upset me that he hadn't filled me in on his plans yet. It wasn't as if he was leaving town. He was moving five blocks away. I should be happy he decided to stay, right?

"Knock, knock," a familiar female voice said from the front door. "I come bearing welcome home gifts."

Lucy hurried past me to open the screen door for Tazia. She was standing there with three bouquets of flowers and a pastry box from the Bird's Eye Bakery. "Oh, Tazia. You shouldn't have," Lucy said, even as she eagerly took the pastry box from her and quickly handed it to my dad.

He'd walked into the room and was gazing at Tazia with a

soft smile. I glanced between them and felt that tingle of magic at my spine that quickly sent warmth through my body.

"Hey. I wondered if you'd stop by," Dad said as he took the bouquets from her hands.

"I couldn't resist bringing flowers over for Lucy." She placed a hand on his forearm and gazed up at him as if he were the only person in the room. The tingle and warmth intensified.

"That was kind of you. I'll get them into some water for her." Dad walked into the kitchen while Tazia stopped near me.

"Marion. I was hoping I'd run into you." She leaned in, giving me a quick kiss on the cheek. "How's business?"

I shrugged. "There haven't been any more disasters, but we haven't exactly had people beating down the door to use our services. Lennon has been teasing her social media page with select details about her dating experience. Most of them are small things to make her audience laugh and keep them engaged, but we haven't yet recovered from the online articles that keep circulating around with all the speculation. Her posts about the entire thing are supposed to drop today. Then we'll see where we are."

She gazed at me, her eyes going unfocused for just a moment. Then she smiled. "I don't think you have anything to worry about."

"I don't?" I asked, wondering what she thought she saw.

"Nope." She squeezed my hand. "Your business will be fine. And in case you haven't noticed, the curse Pixie put on you is fading."

My heart was suddenly in my throat. "It is?"

"It is. Though I'm not sure you'll escape the curse entirely unchanged. You might not be able to see auras the same way."

"Oh." I grimaced. "That would be just my luck."

She chuckled softly. "Live long enough and your luck will change." She winked at me and then went to join my dad in the kitchen. They started chatting like old friends, and Tazia talked about the floral shop she wanted to open in town. It appeared that while she'd been ready to give up the large nursery she'd run before, she wasn't quite ready to retire yet, and this was something manageable.

While the pair worked on arranging the flowers in various vases, I stood next to Lucy and said, "I think if I could see their auras, they'd be a lovely shade of lilac."

"They are," Celia said, once again popping in out of nowhere.

Lucy laughed and turned to her. "You are an amusing one to have around, aren't you?"

"I like to keep things interesting." She blew Lucy a kiss. "Just like you."

Lucy flushed with the compliment and grinned at the ghost.

"Are you headed to *Abs, Buns, and Guns* tonight?" Celia asked Lucy.

"I wouldn't miss it for the world." Lucy made a show of pushing her breasts up to create more cleavage. "I just need to find the right blouse. It's not every day a girl gets to unwrap a package like that."

Celia threw her head back and laughed. "I like you."

"I like you, too, dear." Lucy smiled sweetly at her.

I coughed. "You know it's not a strip club, right?"

"Of course not." Lucy waved an unconcerned hand. "That doesn't mean I won't be unwrapping them with my eyes. It's been a long, long while since I've seen a man who didn't have age spots and wrinkles all over."

"Man, aging is for the birds," Celia said. Then she turned thoughtful. "Though, it is slightly better than the alternative, I suppose."

"You can say that again," Lucy agreed.

I left them to their discussion about *Abs, Buns, and Guns* and went outside to sit on the new wooden swing. I'd only been there for a few minutes when Dad and Tazia walked out. He had his hand on her lower back, and their heads were tilted toward each other as they talked.

I hadn't been intending to eavesdrop, but when dad suddenly turned and looked down at her, his expression was troubled as he said, "I've been touched by darkness, Tazia."

She pressed a gentle hand to his chest. "The antidote to darkness is light, Memphis."

He smiled down at her. "Would you mind joining me on a walk down to the beach? I could use a lot more light in my life."

"I thought you'd never ask."

I watched as they walked back into the house, my heart full of hope.

"Marion?" Jax poked his head out the back door. "There you are. Ready?"

"For you? Always."

He held his hand out to me, and I immediately joined him. We went back inside, said goodbye to Lucy, and then walked two blocks to overlook the ocean. "Do you want to come over after the party tonight?" he asked as he stood behind me, his arms around me.

"Yes." I leaned into him, loving the way I felt when we were together like this. "My dad and Lucy are moving out today. I'm thinking of letting the boys have the apartment above the garage."

"Yeah?" He pressed a soft kiss to my neck. "I bet they'd enjoy a little more privacy."

"They're not the only ones." I turned so we were facing each other and wrapped my hands around his neck. "Now when you spend the night, we don't need to worry so much about waking anyone up."

He chuckled. "Or being woken up by the boys in the next room."

"Ugh, don't remind me." I placed my hands over my ears and shook my head. "Privacy is good for everyone."

His eyes smoldered as he stared down at me, and I immediately took a step back.

"No way, Jax Williams. Don't look at me like that. Not here. Not right now. I have plans tonight and cannot be late."

He glanced at his watch. "Surely you have an hour for me."

I groaned and then stepped back into his arms. "Okay, but just one hour. Not a second more."

"We'll see," he said and quickly led me the couple of blocks to his house. The moment he kicked the door shut, his lips were all over me and clothes were flying.

It was always like that with him. Hot and frenzied. The pure need we shared for each other was unmatched by anyone I'd ever been with before. Just a few days ago, Celia had told me she'd never seen two auras that burned as brightly as ours did for each other. She insisted that when they melded, they were a deep magenta. If that were true, it meant that we were compatible, but it also meant our relationship was ruled by passion.

I'd decided it didn't matter anymore. I'd chosen him and he'd chosen me. The fire was only burning brighter with each passing day. And the more time I spent with him, the more I was convinced he was my forever. And if I'd learned anything being a matchmaker, it was that when two people were determined to be together, nothing could tear them apart.

When Jax had me stripped naked, he picked me up and carried me to his bedroom, and then the world narrowed to the man above me, loving every inch of my body in every way possible.

CHAPTER 29

"*Have* you seen the responses to these posts?" Lennon cried as she waved her phone at me. Her face was alight with happiness, illuminating her beauty from the inside out.

I raised my glass of champagne to her. "The campaign was brilliant," I told her. "Really fantastic, Lennon. Thank you."

Her posts about her experience with Miss Matched Midlife Dating Agency had gone live earlier in the day. She'd been honest about everything that had happened, building a drama-ridden story that ended with me as the hero, saving the love of her life and bringing him back to her just in time for him to save hers.

People online were sharing the story far and wide, and while I still had some haters over the idea that I'd been unethical when dating Jax, most people had gotten over that detail. Our inbox was overflowing again, and when Iris and I got back into the office the next day, we were going to have our work cut out for us going through all the new inquiries.

"No, thank you, Marion. I just can't believe this is my life now." She stood with her glass raised and her white bachelorette veil flowing out behind her. She glanced around at the coven, me, Lucy, and a handful of her friends. "I just want to make a toast to Marion. If it wasn't for her, I wouldn't be marrying the love of my life tomorrow."

"To Marion," everyone said.

"If it wasn't for *me*," Celia said, popping up next to me, "she wouldn't be marrying anyone tomorrow."

I chuckled. "When are you going to let that go?"

"Never."

"Okay. I'll be sure to credit you when I'm asked about it in the next interview," I said with a laugh.

"Don't you dare," she said, shaking her head. "That would ruin the story. Lennon's version is what sells. I just want those who matter to remember it was me who saved the day."

My lips twitched with amusement. "Those who are in the know remember. You can count on that. In fact, I think we make a great team, you and I. We're going to have many great matchmaking years ahead of us."

Celia beamed. Then she quickly sobered. "Not if you don't hold up your end of the bargain. You still owe me a man, remember?"

"Oh, didn't I tell you? I found one." I pointed across the room to where a very attractive man with bulging muscles was floating near the stage. "He used to be one of the dancers, but a tragic accident took his life too soon. Now he hangs out here, watching over his friends and waiting for his own ghostly Ms. Right."

She squinted across the room at the man before turning back to me. "Are you shitting me? This is for real?"

I nodded. "Very real. He's waiting for you to go introduce yourself."

"Wait, why isn't he coming over here?" she asked, suspicion in her tone.

"He's a little shy. The shy silent type." I grinned at her. "Go on, Celia. What are you waiting for?"

"I... I don't know." She fluffed her hair and straightened her clothes before starting to float over, but then she paused. "How did you find him?"

"I had a little help from Grace and Gigi. He was haunting this place but hadn't figured out how to harness his energy to be present like you are. Now go before his lights fade out."

"Thank you," she said. A moment later, she was floating beside Danny, running her hands over his chest and smiling up at him with hearts in her eyes.

"They make a cute couple."

I grinned, recognizing Tandy Knight's voice. "When did you get here?"

She stepped up beside me, holding out a cocktail. I took it, knowing it was a Moscow Mule, and ditched the champagne.

"Ten minutes ago." She pressed her glass to mine and said, "To Marion."

"Stop," I said, laughing, but completed her toast and took a sip. "Does Lennon know you're here?"

"Yeah. I just said hello. We're signing the contracts tomorrow. I can't wait to get her on air. That woman is gold."

"You're not wrong about that." After all the trauma Lennon had gone through because of me and my stalker, I hadn't waited to facilitate the meeting with Tandy. I'd made the call a few days after the surfing incident and things had moved fast after that. Tandy had come to Premonition Pointe for the meeting and had made her decision that day. Ever since, they'd been in contract negotiations. "She's radiant. People are drawn to that."

"That's what I'm counting on." Tandy slipped her arm through mine, and we stood there watching everyone have a good time until the lights went down and the *Abs, Buns, and Guns* show started.

Tandy was fully into it as I knew she would be. She took off toward the stage, waving money and trying to direct them to interact with Lennon. One of them did, making the group go wild. I spotted Celia, completely wrapped up in Danny, ignoring the show she'd desperately pushed for. The coven was sitting back enjoying the shenanigans with only Carly getting a little wild, waving her dollar bills in the air.

I was grinning and watching my friends have a great time being silly when someone touched my elbow.

"Marion Matched?" the man said.

"Yes?" I turned to him, frowning. He wasn't wearing a shirt with the company's logo like all the other employees. In fact, he shifted from foot to foot, appearing uncomfortable.

"I need to talk to you. It's an emergency," he said, gesturing to the door. "Can we go outside where it's a little quieter?"

I wasn't in the habit of walking off with men I didn't know, but this one looked vaguely familiar. I followed him to the door that led to the outdoor smoking area. Because the show had just started, it was empty. "Do I know you?"

He shook his head. "No, I'm Hollister Crooner, but you know my brother. Garrison Crooner. He's engaged—"

"To Kiera Ho—I mean Vincent. Kiera Vincent."

"That's right. She went missing forty-eight hours ago. She told Garrison if anything ever happened to her to call you."

My blood ran cold. "Kiera's missing?"

He nodded.

I quickly sent a text to Iris, telling her there was an emergency and to meet me outside. We had a former client who was missing, and I was the only one who could find her.

DEANNA'S BOOK LIST

Witches of Keating Hollow:
Soul of the Witch
Heart of the Witch
Spirit of the Witch
Dreams of the Witch
Courage of the Witch
Love of the Witch
Power of the Witch
Essence of the Witch
Muse of the Witch
Vision of the Witch
Waking of the Witch
Honor of the Witch
Promise of the Witch

Witches of Christmas Grove:
A Witch For Mr. Holiday
A Witch For Mr. Christmas
A Witch For Mr. Winter

A Witch For Mr. Mistletoe

Premonition Pointe Novels:
Witching For Grace
Witching For Hope
Witching For Joy
Witching For Clarity
Witching For Moxie
Witching For Kismet

Miss Matched Midlife Dating Agency:
Star-crossed Witch
Honor-bound Witch
Outmatched Witch

Jade Calhoun Novels:
Haunted on Bourbon Street
Witches of Bourbon Street
Demons of Bourbon Street
Angels of Bourbon Street
Shadows of Bourbon Street
Incubus of Bourbon Street
Bewitched on Bourbon Street
Hexed on Bourbon Street
Dragons of Bourbon Street

Pyper Rayne Novels:
Spirits, Stilettos, and a Silver Bustier
Spirits, Rock Stars, and a Midnight Chocolate Bar
Spirits, Beignets, and a Bayou Biker Gang
Spirits, Diamonds, and a Drive-thru Daiquiri Stand
Spirits, Spells, and Wedding Bells

Ida May Chronicles:
Witched To Death
Witch, Please
Stop Your Witchin'

Crescent City Fae Novels:
Influential Magic
Irresistible Magic
Intoxicating Magic

Last Witch Standing:
Bewitched by Moonlight
Soulless at Sunset
Bloodlust By Midnight
Bitten At Daybreak

Witch Island Brides:
The Wolf's New Year Bride
The Vampire's Last Dance
The Warlock's Enchanted Kiss
The Shifter's First Bite

Destiny Novels:
Defining Destiny
Accepting Fate

Wolves of the Rising Sun:
Jace
Aiden
Luc
Craved
Silas

Darien
Wren

Black Bear Outlaws:
Cyrus
Chase
Cole

Bayou Springs Alien Mail Order Brides:
Zeke
Gunn
Echo

ABOUT THE AUTHOR

New York Times and USA Today bestselling author, Deanna Chase, is a native Californian, transplanted to the slower paced lifestyle of southeastern Louisiana. When she isn't writing, she is often goofing off with her husband in New Orleans or playing with her two shih tzu dogs. For more information and updates on newest releases visit her website at deannachase.com.

Made in United States
Troutdale, OR
12/23/2023

16389105R00152